GRANDADDY'S STORIES

By

Richard McLawhorn

Art work & Illustrations by
Richard McLawhorn

Trafford

Publishing Inc.

Order this book online at www.trafford.com
or email orders@trafford.com

Most Trafford titles are also available at major online book retailers.

Printed in Victoria, BC, Canada.

ISBN: 978-1-4269-0641-1 (sc)

*Our mission is to efficiently provide the world's finest, most comprehensive book publishing
service, enabling every author to experience success. To find out how to publish your book, your
way, and have it available worldwide, visit us online at www.trafford.com*

Trafford rev. 11/13/2009

 www.trafford.com

North America & international
toll-free: 1 888 232 4444 (USA & Canada)
phone: 250 383 6864 ♦ fax: 812 355 4082

A Word from the Author

This is a collection of narratives from an old man who entertained and enlightened his grandchildren during their visits to his home in rural North Carolina. After the man's death, the stories were collected, edited, and published by one of his grandsons.

The grandfather and the grandson are fictitious characters. Neither resembles nor represents my grandfather, my grandsons, or me.

This book is intended to provide entertainment for people who are fond of history but whose reading habits do not normally include more scholarly and more protracted works. I hope you enjoy it.

Richard McLawhorn
© 2009

A Note of Appreciation

This book is based on my research as a graduate student at East Carolina University from 1987-1991. I would like to express my appreciation for the guidance I received during that time from the faculty of the Department of History. I am especially indebted to Anthony J. Papalas, Professor, and Carl E. Swanson, Associate Professor, both excellent teachers and true scholars.

RM

TABLE OF CONTENTS

GRANDADDY'S STORIES

I fondly recall many cold winter afternoons at the feet of my grandfather, listening to his stories. My sister, my brother, and my cousins knelt with me or lay on their stomachs on the multi-colored oval rug next to the old wood stove and watched the darkness settle on the barnyard outside as we heard ancient tales of adventure and romance and of treachery and barbaric warfare. A few of the heroes of my grandfather's stories exhibited courage and compassion as well as wisdom and wit. Some of his villains were foolish and egotistical, or mean-spirited, or bloodthirsty. But most of his characters were human beings with traits that we admired as well as weaknesses that either saddened us or made us laugh.

My grandfather breathed life into those long-dead spirits and coaxed them into his little den next to the kitchen of that old farm house that smelled of all the chicken and potatoes and corn bread my grandmother, her mother, and her grandmother had fried and boiled and baked through the years. We sat spellbound as he summoned his apparitions from the deserts of Asia, from the commercial centers of Europe, from misty-blue islands of the Mediterranean, and from the early towns and villages of colonial North America. They arrived from both the distant and the not-too-distant past, and we left behind the smell of oak wood burning in the old woodstove and the banging of the hog feeders in the barnyard and the whining and scratching of the bird dogs on the back porch. We followed him to another world as we inhaled the sights and sounds and smells of ancient times. Our grandfather's magic connected us to his stories' characters and wove them into the fabric of the long, ongoing record of mankind.

Sometimes his audience was small. On occasions, my sister and I had my grandfather to ourselves, when our cousins weren't around and before the baby was old enough to understand and to be trusted near the stove. But the size of Grandaddy's audience didn't matter. Just one of his eight grandchildren was enough to send him back to the past for another

1

yarn. In summer we sat and clung to the porch swing and floated to and fro as he imparted his tales from his rocking chair, ignoring the swing's tiny squeal of protest each time it paused at the top of its arc and prepared to reverse direction. While we listened, Grandmama came out to serve brownies or peanut butter crackers and iced tea or lemonade. Sometimes we sat on the shady bank of the farm pond, grasping a bamboo fishing pole in one hand and slapping mosquitoes with the other.

As I listen to the audio tapes that have preserved his voice, I am in awe of my grandfather's ability to recall details of these ancient tales as if he had been an eyewitness. I remember as a child being entertained by both his delivery and his ability to pull one story after another from his stockpile. According to my grandmother, he was always an avid reader, but his storytelling began after he enrolled in two history courses for fun at the local community college. He began by telling his stories to his buddies around a pot of fish stew with a beer in his hand. I know that some of the stories are true. For others, however, he relied on the words of ancient writers who, in some cases, passed along accounts from previous generations. In any case, and as I researched the stories, I marveled at the level of accuracy of even the smallest details.

Grandaddy's stories are alive today in the minds of my cousins and my siblings and me. We still make an occasional reference to Raleigh's fateful trip up the Orinoco River, or Josepheus' predictions of the next emperor of Rome, or midnight visits from Stalin's secret police.

My grandfather is gone now, but, fortunately, I discovered my audio recordings a few years ago stowed away for future generations. Those recordings are the basis for this collection. The text appears almost word-for-word as he told it. I edited only to elaborate on certain passages for the sake of clarity. I hope you enjoy these stories as much as we, the grandchildren, did.

A KNIGHT'S TALE: THE COLORFUL LIFE AND TIMES OF SIR WALTER RALEIGH

A note from the grandson:

THE RENAISSANCE

The expansion of international commercial activity around the Mediterranean in the fourteenth and fifteenth centuries created a period of prosperity for the leading cities of Italy. This wealth helped to create a new era of European thought and imagination and a renewed interest in art and philosophy and education. This period, which we call the Renaissance, produced great works of art and literature, awakened an interest in science and exploration, and renewed man's appreciation for the power of his genius. Classical manuscripts were translated from Greek and Latin to local languages. As the Italian people migrated from the countryside to urban centers, cities such as Florence, Venice, Padua, Milan, Genoa, and Rome grew and prospered. From this taste of economic freedom, the cities' inhabitants developed an appreciation for individual freedom and a sense of loyalty to the society that allowed and protected that freedom. The works of Michelangelo, Leonardo, Dante, Petrarch, Boccaccio, and Machiavelli are familiar examples of the art and literature of the Italian Renaissance.

Within the next century the commercial activity and the renewed appreciation for art and education spread to northern Europe and to Britain. The wealth created by commerce produced a demand for products from outside Europe. Spices such as cinnamon, nutmeg, cloves, and ginger and black pepper, perfumes, and silks were in great demand. The promise of huge profits to be earned for delivering these luxuries to the Europeans spurred a race to find an oceanic route to Asia.

After decades of exploration the Portuguese established trade routes to Asia by working their way around the continent of Africa. In 1492, Spanish monarchs financed the voyage of Christopher Columbus to find a route to the East by sailing west. Columbus and his men never made their way to Asia. Instead, they discovered two continents that had been previously unknown to Europeans, and, among the fruits of subsequent expeditions by other Spanish explorers were huge deposits of gold and silver in both Mexico and Peru.

In 1588, Elizabeth, daughter of Henry VIII, was crowned Queen of England. As she took the throne, the Spanish were shipping enormous shiploads of gold and silver from the new world to Spain, and Spain had become the greatest economic and military power on earth.

My grandfather tells the story of a contemporary of Queen Elizabeth and one of her top administrators, Sir Walter Raleigh.

TWO STORIES

This time, I'm going to tell you two stories in one. One story is about an ambitious man who didn't mind stepping on toes to get ahead and who loved to sail the seas and to fight. He was always looking for a gold mine or some way to get rich quick. He was a man who liked to read and write poetry and write about history. He was a smooth talker who got his way with women, especially Queen Elizabeth, the Queen of England. His name was Walter Raleigh, and after he was knighted by the Queen, he became Sir Walter Raleigh, just like Sir Sean Connery and Sir Paul McCartney and Sir Arthur Conan Doyle, the man who wrote the Sherlock Holmes stories.

Some historians say Sir Walter was England's first Renaissance man. I guess they say that because he had good manners and was always well dressed and loved music and poetry. And, because he had a good education and was interested in science and philosophy. And, because he was a soldier, fearless in battle. And, because he had vision and was a smooth talker who knew how to talk others into sharing his vision. So, I suppose he was as much a Renaissance man as anybody was. But he had his faults. He was as greedy as he could be, and he thought he was hot you-know-what on a stick. It was like they printed him a special dictionary and they left out the word humility.

The other story is about the first English colony in North America. They call this the Lost Colony. This was one of Sir Walter's many ventures, and it was one of the ones that failed.

First, I'll tell you a little about Walter's background. Now if you remember, ever since way back in mediaeval times, the oldest son inherited the castle and all his daddy's land, and all the other sons didn't get anything but maybe a horse and some traveling money. Once they were grown, they didn't have any choice but to leave home and become soldiers or study to be priests. What the daughters did was to look for other oldest sons to marry.

Young Walter was one of those young men in that boat. He was not the oldest boy. But his father didn't have much land or money, anyway, so it really didn't matter. Besides, Walter was born in a time when there were plenty of exciting

5

ways to try to get rich in the world. America had been discovered just sixty years or so before he was born, and a lot of young men from Europe were sailing over there to try to find gold or try to help rob a Spanish treasure ship or just see what was there. None of them were looking for free land, though, where they could settle down and raise some crops and build a plantation in the wilderness. Not yet. That would come later.

Young Walter was born in either 1552 or 1554. Nobody knows for sure. He was born and raised in Devon. Devon is a section of England that sticks out into the Atlantic Ocean. You know, Britain is just an island off the coast of Europe anyway, and so England has always been known for doing a lot of trading and traveling across the water and for having a large navy. Well, Devon was known for its seamen. Walter had two half brothers who were sea captains. Their names were Sir Humphrey Gilbert and Sir John Gilbert. Another great sea captain, Sir Richard Grenville and the most famous of all, Sir Francis Drake, were both supposedly Walter's cousins. I'm not sure if I believe all that, but, anyway, you can see that Walter had been around plenty of men who had traveled and explored and been in and out of plenty of dangerous situations.

COLUMBUS' DISCOVERY

Like I said, this was an exciting time for people that loved to just sail around and look for adventure and look for ways to get rich. Columbus had accidentally discovered the Americas in 1492. He had been trying to find a new route to Asia. Instead, he landed on land that the people in Europe didn't even know about. This new land turned out to be more than twice size of all of Europe put together. In the next few years, other explorers from Spain had discovered just how big all these two continents over here were. And everywhere they went, they claimed the new land to be owned by Spain. Pretty soon Spain owned Mexico, Florida, a bunch of islands in the Caribbean Sea, and almost all of South America. The main thing they were looking for was gold, and they found plenty of it, and silver, too.

THE INDIANS

Before the Spanish came, there were all kinds of people who lived in North America and South America. When Columbus landed in those islands in the Caribbean Sea, he and his crew thought they had landed in the East Indies off the coast of India. So they started calling the people there Indians. In fact, he made three more trips to the Caribbean in the next few years before he died, and he never found out that he had discovered these two new continents. Anyway, Columbus' name for the people in the Americas took hold. So we still call native Americans Indians today.

Not all of these native people were alike. In fact, they couldn't have been more different. Some of them lived quietly in peace, and some liked to attack other tribes and take their food and tools and their women. Some were poor, and some lived in great cities and wore fancy clothes and gold jewelry. Indians in Mexico traded with Indians way down in South America and way up in New York and Illinois. The Indians walked everywhere they went because there weren't any horses in the Americas. They also didn't have cattle, hogs, chickens, or sheep. They got their meat from squirrels, deer, rabbits, bears, and turkeys, and some tribes liked dog meat.

Indians also had never seen wheat, rice, cabbage, honey, peaches, pears, oranges, or olives before the Spanish came. But they had some foods that the people in Europe had never heard of. Some of the new foods the Spanish found over here and took back home with them were corn, potatoes, sweet potatoes, tomatoes, chocolate, vanilla, all kinds of beans, squash, pumpkins, peanuts, and pecans. That, right there, was worth all Columbus' trouble. Not to mention turkeys.

The worst thing the Spanish and other Europeans brought

with them was diphtheria, measles, small pox, and other diseases. The Indians had no immunity whatsoever because they had never been exposed to any of these. So epidemics spread from one village to another, and we don't know how bad it was, but we know it was bad. Somebody said they thought maybe up to two thirds of all the Indians died from diseases brought from Europe.

SLAVERY IN THE AMERICAS

Anyway, the Spanish came, and some Indians tried to get along with them at first, and some were afraid of them. If you think about it, the Indians had never seen horses, and these Spaniards came riding up with armor on and armor on their horses, and they had these long metal swords and lances. So when some Indians tried to fight the Spanish, they never stood a chance. The Spanish needed workers to work in the mines, so they rode in and attacked villages and towns and captured the young men and made them into slaves.

Before Columbus sailed off across the Atlantic Ocean looking for a new way to get to Asia, the Portuguese had been doing the same thing. They had been sailing down the coast of Africa looking for that bottom tip so they could turn left and sail over to Asia and do some trading. But Africa was a lot bigger than they thought, and it took them years and years to reach that southern tip. In the meantime, they had established trading posts along the shore of Africa. Anyway, it wasn't long before they started capturing young Africans and hauling them over to the Americas and selling them for slaves. That's how the first Africans came to America and how the curse of slavery first got started over here. And this curse led to a terrible, bloody civil war between the people of the United States three hundred years later. And even today, there's still a lot of hard feelings about slavery and that war and what happened afterward. But that's another story.

SPANISH TREASURE SHIPS

Let's go back to these two new continents that Columbus had discovered. The Spanish explorers had taken over the Indians' gold mines and silver mines in Mexico and Peru, and they were hauling all these shiploads of gold and silver back to Spain. Before long Spain had become the richest nation in the world. Of course, there weren't many nations in the world at this time. Nationhood was a pretty new idea. Most of the world was made up of tribes or city-states, or small kingdoms like the ones in Germany and Italy. Spain was one of the first unified nations. Then there was Britain, and there was France, and there was the Netherlands. And they were all jealous of Spain and all that land they owned in America with all the gold and silver mines.

So these Spanish treasure ships became targets. Just about every ship that went down to the Caribbean Sea had a crew full of hard-fighting, greedy, blood-thirsty pirates, and they were looking for these Spanish treasure ships. A lot of times the captains of these pirate ships were those second and third sons of the noble families in Europe. Sometimes they would go before their king or queen and ask for enough money to buy their ships and weapons and supplies. Then they wouldn't be called pirates. They'd be called privateers.

The privateers would round up a crew and head down to the Caribbean and hide behind some island and wait for a Spanish treasure ship to come by. It was not as easy as you might think, though, because the Spanish started sending their ships in convoys, under the protection of warships of the Spanish navy. Anyway, if the privateers were able to capture a Spanish ship, they would leave the Spanish crew on an island and sail the Spanish ship back home or either load the gold on their own ship and sink the Spanish ship. When they got home they would turn over half the gold to the king or queen and give each crew member a share. That was the crew's pay.

Queen Elizabeth secretly sent her English sea captains such as Sir Francis Drake, Sir Humphrey Gilbert, and Sir John Hawkins out to capture Spanish treasure ships, even though England was not at war with Spain. The English sea captains became very good at it. They got to be heroes, and they were known as the "sea dogs" back home.

The name of Sir Francis Drake was feared by the Spanish. They called him "the dragon." He was known to hold entire towns on the coast of Mexico hostage by threatening to bombard the towns if they didn't turn over their gold to him. Later on he sailed all the way around the world and attacked Spanish towns on the Pacific side. He was the first English sea captain to sail around the world.

TRADE ROUTES

Finding the Spanish ships was not as hard as you might think. They had a certain route that they followed just like all the other sailing ships back then. The prevailing winds move in a circle, south down the coast of Africa, then west to the northern coast of South America, then north up the coast of Mexico and Florida, then east to Europe. South of the equator, they make a circle in the opposite direction. Anyway, Saint Augustine, Florida, was the Spanish ships' last stop for food and water before heading for Spain.

WALTER RALEIGH

Now, let's get back to young Walter Raleigh. His family sent him to this famous university named Oxford, but he dropped out after a year and joined an army of French Huguenots who were fighting the Catholics over in France. The French Huguenots were Protestants, and they were over there fighting the Catholics. Wars between Protestants and Catholics were pretty common back then. Protestant religious groups had just sprung up a few decades before, and there had been fighting and killing ever since. In fact, that's one reason why the English hated the Spanish and why the English hated the Irish so much. The Spanish and the Irish were Catholic and the English were Protestant.

Anyway, when Sir Walter Raleigh came back from the wars in the Netherlands, his half-brother, Sir Humphrey Gilbert, offered him a job as a captain of one of his ships. Sir Humphrey had seven ships, and they sailed out across the Atlantic to look for land for England and gold. But a big storm blew up and they all got separated, then they were attacked by the Spanish, and they finally returned home with damaged ships and without ever making it to America.

Then Raleigh joined the army and went to Ireland to fight the Irish rebels. They made him a captain in the army, and he turned out to be a good leader and a tough soldier, but there were stories about how he and his men executed a bunch of unarmed prisoners.

Anyway, when he returned home, the Queen had heard about him and she sent for him and she liked him, so he stayed in London and became one of her favorite advisors and maybe more. We don't know about that for sure. We do know that he got to be in charge of all the licenses for anyone to sell wine or cloth in England, and he became a judge for the tin mines in Cornwall. That's how he became rich. He was also elected to Parliament, and Queen Elizabeth knighted him and appointed him captain of her personal guard.

Meanwhile, half-brother Gilbert was planning another voyage to establish a colony in North America. He had a contract with the Queen. They had decided to try to establish a fort somewhere north of Florida that they could use as a base for attacking Spanish treasure ships. Raleigh's position in London was too important, though, and the Queen ordered Raleigh to stay behind. Well, Sir Humphrey made it over to Newfoundland, up in Canada, but a big storm blew

11

up once again, and several of his ships were wrecked and sank including the one he was on. He and all the crew members on his ship were drowned.

When Raleigh heard his half-brother was dead, he asked the Queen for Sir Humphrey's contract to start an English colony in North America, and she gave it to him. The next year Raleigh sent his own two ships over to explore the coastline and find a good spot for a colony. His party was led by two captains. Their names were Phillip Amadas and Arthur Barlowe. Years earlier the French had tried to establish a colony down about where Charleston, South Carolina, is now, but they had been wiped out by the Spanish. So Raleigh wanted to locate his colony some distance from Florida. On the other hand, he didn't want it way up in Newfoundland in the middle of nowhere. So they were looking somewhere in between, and they found Roanoke Island on the coast of North Carolina.

Amadas and Barlowe's soldiers landed and stayed for several weeks and traded with the Indians on the island, and they persuaded two of the braves to return to England with them. The Indians were from the Roanoak tribe, and they spoke an Indian language called Algonqian. The two who went to England were named Manteo and Wanchese. Sir Walter Raleigh introduced   them to the Queen. Today the county seat of Dare County is Manteo, and one of the towns close by is Wanchese. They are both located on Roanoke Island.

THE FIRST COLONY

Sir Walter was so pleased with the report from Amadas and Barlowe that the next April he sent seven ships with men and supplies and the two Indians to establish a colony at Roanoke Island. When Sir Walter Raleigh got excited about something, he didn't mess around. It was 1585. On the way over, a storm came up and the ships got separated. After the storm was over, some of them met up in Puerto Rico, and they waited weeks and weeks for the others. The rest of the ships never came. Finally they sailed on up to Roanoke with the ships they had, and the other ships did finally meet them there. Anyway, that's why they were so late getting there that summer.

Then, when they got there, they found that the harbor was too shallow for the bigger ships, and they had to anchor out in the ocean. The biggest ship was grounded on the bottom, and the waves pounded until it broke apart, so they lost a whole ship's cargo of supplies. The captain, Sir Richard Grenville, decided that he needed to return to England for more supplies, so he sailed for home on August 25. He took 200 of the men with him so the ones left behind wouldn't run out of food as quick. On his way home, Sir Richard took the time to go hunting, and he found himself a large Spanish ship with a valuable cargo. So he went home a hero, and Sir Walter sold the Spanish cargo for enough money to pay for the whole colony.

Meanwhile, back in Roanoke, the colonists were not doing too well. The leader was Colonel Ralph Lane. He had 107 men with him, and all of them were soldiers. They didn't have one farmer or fisherman or hunter among them. They did have an artist named John White and a scientist and map-maker named Thomas Hariot, but Ralph Lane was a know-it-all, and he didn't listen. He and the soldiers had spent all their time searching for gold. They had traveled far and wide in their search. Some had gone as far as the Chesapeake Bay. And now winter had come and they had run out of food. They had stolen from the Indians and gotten into a fight with them and killed some of them and burned one of their villages. They even chopped off the chief's head. Now they were starving.

Then Sir Francis Drake dropped by on his way to England. He was on his way home with 27 ships, and several of them were loaded with cargoes of captured treasure. He had stopped to see how the new colony was doing. Well, Ralph Lane said they were not doing well at all, and Sir Francis offered to leave them a ship and enough food to last them another couple of months. That way they could hold out maybe until Sir Richard Greenville arrived, or they could go ahead and sail home if they had to.

Before they could get everything together, though, a huge storm blew up. It lasted three days. When it was over, several of the ships had been destroyed. Others had taken off to get away from the storm, and nobody knew if they had survived or not. A lot of the supplies had been sunk or ruined. Ralph Lane and his men decided they were ready to go home, the quicker the better. So Sir Francis Drake loaded them aboard and they got ready to head for home.

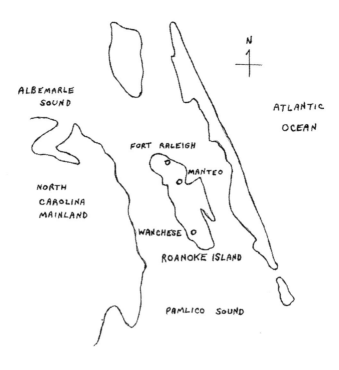

They sent a boat back to pick up the men left on Roanoke Island to guard the fort. The sea was still rough, and water was splashing into the boat, and it was hard to row and hard to steer. The boat ran aground several times on their way back to the ships. When it did, they'd have to jump out, push the boat back into deeper water, and jump back in. A lot of the personal belongings from the fort were lost overboard including quite a few of John White's drawings. The men were so anxious to get back to the ships anchored out at sea that they left three men behind. Those three must have been out in the woods hunting or something, but with the storm brewing and all, Sir Francis didn't have time to go look for them.

A few days after Drake and all the men from the colony sailed away, guess what happened. You probably guessed it. Sir Richard Grenville arrived with all the supplies the colony needed. Then, when he couldn't find anyone, he didn't know what to do. So he left 15 men there at the fort, and he sailed back to England. He never did find the three men that Ralph Lane had left behind, and no one knows what happened to them.

THE SECOND COLONY

Well, you can imagine how angry Sir Walter was when he saw Ralph Lane and his soldiers come shuffling in to report to him once they got back to England. And then, two weeks later, here comes Grenville with three ships still loaded down with supplies. Sir Walter Raleigh was fit to be tied. He told all of them that if he had gone with them, they wouldn't have come back. He was real disappointed.

But he was a hard-headed man, and he didn't give up. When he finally cooled down, he started to thinking about plans for sending another colony over the next spring. John White told him he should send families instead of soldiers. That way they would start farms and put down roots. He also told him that next time they should build their village on the Chesapeake Bay where there was plenty of deep water so you could tie up your

15

ships to a tree on the bank.

What John White was saying made sense to Sir Walter. So he told John White to start advertising and for him to offer each family willing to go and settle in Virginia 500 acres of land. He decided to make John White the governor of the new colony. They ended up with 150 men. A lot of them were taking their wives with them, and some of them had children. One of the couples was Eleanor White Dare, the Governor's daughter, and her husband, Ananias Dare. I don't know who his parents were or why they named him that, but I imagine he was teased about it when he was growing up. Anyway, Eleanor was a tough woman because she was carrying a baby during the trip over and she gave birth not long after they arrived. It was a girl, and they named her Virginia Dare.

They sailed over in three ships, and the man in charge of the ships was a man named Simon Fernandez. Simon was a Portuguese navigator who had been sailing ships for the British for years. He was kind of a sneaky fellow and he was real greedy. He had sailed with several of those old sea dogs and had spent a lot of time attacking Spanish treasure ships. And that is what he wanted to do this time instead of being a nursemaid to a bunch of women and children. So you can see why John White didn't like him. In fact, Mr. White and Mr. Fernandez hated one another. They argued over everything. Remember when I told you about the prevailing winds making a big circle? Well, they went by Puerto Rico on the way to Virginia and they needed to stop for water and meat and salt, but they couldn't agree on where to stop. Whenever Simon decided to stop at a place, if they couldn't find water or salt or sheep or some other animal there, John White would blame it on Simon Fernandez. John White kept a diary, and he wrote down all Simon's mistakes to show how incompetent he was.

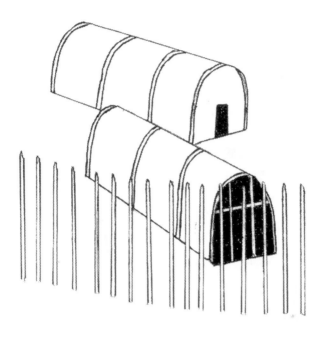

ABANDONED ON ROANOKE ISLAND

So when they finally arrived at Roanoke Island and dropped anchor off the coast, John White and a lot of the settlers took a boat over to the island. They wanted to check on the 15 men that Sir Richard Grenville had left to guard the fort when he and the others had returned to England the previous year.

After John White and his men had left the ship, Simon Fernandez told his sailors not to bring them back. He was refusing to let the settlers come back on board. So, instead of continuing on up to the Chesapeake Bay to start a new settlement, John White and the families were stuck there on Roanoke Island, and there was not one thing John White could do about it. Simon was deliberately disobeying Sir Raleigh's orders. He planned to head back home and to hunt for Spanish treasure ships on the way.

Well, they never did find out what happened to the 15 men that had been left behind the year before. John White and his men, after they found out that they were stuck at Roanoke, went down to the town that Ralph Lane and his men had built the year before. The fort had been torn down, but the houses were still in good shape, even though the weeds had grown up all around and the houses were covered by vines. There was one set of bones from one of the soldiers who was killed. Later on some friendly Indians would tell them about the other 14. They said that the Roanoaks had attacked the fort and killed two of the English soldiers, but the other 13 had escaped in a boat. So I guess we'll never know what happened to them.

MANTEO AND WANCHESE

Now I want to tell you about Manteo and Wanchese, the two Indians that went to England with Amadas and Barlowe two years before. When they came back to America with Ralph Lane in 1585, Wanchese went back to live with his own people. He didn't like the English very much. Manteo, though, was a good friend of John White, and he stayed with the English. He wore English clothes and had himself a sword and a pistol. He went back to England when Ralph Lane did, and he came back to America again with John White. Now, Manteo was not really an original member of the Roanoak tribe. He had come from over in Hatteras, and he was living with the Roanoaks at the time. He was a member of the Croatoan tribe. Both tribes spoke the Algonqian language, and they were neighbors and friends.

The reason I'm telling you all this is so you'll understand the situation in the Roanoke area when John White and his colonists got put ashore there. Remember, Ralph Lane and his dastardly men had attacked several Roanoak Indian villages and burned one down and killed their chief, Wingina, and cut his head off. When they did that, they made some permanent enemies, and one of them was Wanchese.

THE DEATH OF GEORGE HOWE

Well, when John White and his colonists found out they were stuck at Roanoke Island, they posted guards all around because they knew that Ralph Lane's men had ruined any chance of making friends with the Roanoaks again. But then, two weeks went by and they hadn't seen any signs of Indians, so they began to feel a little better about it. Then one day one of the men named George Howe went crabbing by himself. He was out in the water with his shirt and pants and boots off with a forked stick to catch the crabs with. Then, suddenly, Wanchese and his braves came charging out of the woods and shot him 16 times with arrows and then dragged him up on the bank and beat his head in.

THE CROATOANS

You can imagine how this made those English people feel, with women and young children, out in the wilderness, 5,000 miles from home. After they got over the shock two days later, Manteo offered to take some of them in a boat over to Hatteras to talk to some of his fellow Croatoans to find out more about what the Roanoaks were up to. When the Croatoans first saw Manteo and the white men, they went and got their weapons because Ralph Lane had attacked them by mistake one time before. But pretty soon Manteo and the settlers had smoothed things out with them, and they sat down and ate and spent the night and talked some more the next day. The Croatoans promised that they would talk to the Roanoaks and apologize for what Ralph Lane had done and then they would let the settlers know what kind of reaction the Roanoaks had.

RETALIATION

So the settlers went back to their village on Roanoke and reported all this to John White and the others. Then they waited to hear from the Croatoans. A week passed, though, and they didn't hear anything. Meanwhile, George Howe's family and friends were angry about what the Indians had done to old George, and they didn't want a truce. They wanted revenge. They wanted to teach the Indians that they couldn't get away with killing a white man.

They decided to send 25 men over to the mainland to attack the Roanoak village. John White didn't agree with this decision, but he couldn't stop his men. They took boats over in the middle of the night and snuck in and attacked at dawn. The Indians all ran out into the marsh with the English men chasing and shooting. One Indian was killed before the colonists realized that they had attacked the Croatoans by mistake. The Croatoans had come over to gather up corn left behind by the Roanoaks. The Roanoaks had pulled up stakes and left their village behind after they had killed George Howe.

When they realized what the men had done, John White and Manteo were greatly distressed, as you would expect. Manteo had taken part in the raid, and he partially blamed himself for the mistake. John White knew that now they could never make friends with the local Indians again. He decided that they needed to migrate on up to the Chesapeake Bay the next year. He also knew he needed to send for more supplies to get them through the winter. He started asking around for volunteers to go to England for supplies.

A few days after the raid on the wrong Indians, the colonists held a celebration for their friend, Manteo. The christened him and gave him a title, Lord of Roanoke Island.

Then, about a week later John White became a grandfather. They named her Virginia, and Eleanor White had married a Dare, so the baby's name was Virginia Dare.

RETURN TO ENGLAND

John White couldn't find anyone who wanted to go back to England for supplies. The settlers sent a committee to talk to John White and to request that he go himself. He thought he was the last one that needed to go. He didn't want to leave his daughter and new granddaughter, and he thought the people needed his leadership. After all, he had already been through one hard winter there. Plus, he wanted to get started on their plans to move the colony on up to the north.

But the people kept begging him to go. They said he was the only one with enough clout to get what they needed and to bring back more families. The more people they had the more security they had and the more help they had doing all the work that needed to be done.

So John White went. And it was a rough voyage home. Most of the crew got sick. Some died. And a big storm blew up and pushed them in the wrong direction for six days. They finally ended up in Ireland, and they got fresh supplies and made it home a few days later. It had taken seven hard weeks or more to get home.

WAR WITH SPAIN

Meanwhile, the Spanish king had gotten real tired of his ships and his towns in Mexico being attacked, and now he heard that the English had started to put colonies in North America. So he decided to deal with England once and for all. He had plenty of money, so he ordered his ship-builders to start building big warships. They built the biggest fleet of warships the world had ever seen.

So the English had started to prepare for a major attack when John White arrived in England. But he and Sir Walter were able to pull some strings and put together seven ships with supplies and more colonists to take back to Roanoke the next March. But before they could get underway, the navy sent word that they needed every available warship for the battle that was coming up with Spain. They did say that John White could have two small ships and a few crewmen to take his colonists and supplies back to Virginia.

Well, the voyage back to Roanoke was a disaster. The captain and the crew of his little ship were not in any big hurry to get to America. They were looking for loot, and they tried to attack every ship they saw that wasn't English. Finally, they were attacked themselves by two French ships. The French sailors came aboard, and there was a big fight. John White and almost all the Englishmen were wounded, and the French took all their supplies and all their personal belongings. When the French left, there was not a thing they could do but return to England.

After that, John White had to give up on returning to his colony at Roanoke until after the war with Spain was over.

THE SPANISH ARMADA

One day in the summer of 1588, the gigantic Spanish fleet finally sailed out into the Atlantic Ocean. They were sailing toward England, ready for battle. Can you imagine what an impression 130 large warships made, sailing along in formation, ships as far as you could see on the horizon? Most of them were brand new. They had been constructed especially for this attack on England. Each ship had rows of great big cannons lined up on each side. They were called the Spanish Armada. They had eight thousand sailors and nineteen thousand soldiers on board. This would be the biggest naval battle that had ever taken place in the history of the world.

The English had 200 ships, all sizes and all shapes, kind of a hodge-podge, really. There were sixteen thousand English sailors on those ships. For the most part, the English ships were not as big and their cannons were not as big as the ones the Spanish had, but the English ships were faster, and they could duck around and make sharp turns.

They had three battles that first day, and neither side had much damage. It started when the Spanish ships sailed in all bunched up, and the English ships couldn't get between them. After the third battle, the Spanish headed back to France and entered a French harbor for the night.

That night the English set some ships on fire and sailed them into the harbor to crash into the Spanish ships. The Spanish panicked and cut their anchor lines and sailed out to the open sea. In all the confusion, the English ships attacked early the next morning and destroyed several of the Spanish ships. Then a big storm blew up, and the Spanish ships sailed away in all directions. Some of them sailed all the way up and around Scotland and Ireland. When the Spanish fleet got back home, they didn't have but 80 of their 130 ships left. From then on, on up into the twentieth century, the British were known to have the biggest and best navy in the world. After that, Britain was known as the Mistress of the Seas.

JOHN WHITE RETURNS TO ROANOKE

A year and a half more passed before John White was able to persuade some people to finance another trip to Roanoke. There were three ships in this expedition, and he was not in charge. Once more, it was the same old story. The captains of the three ships and their crews were more interested in capturing Spanish ships than they were in going to Roanoke. So they sailed down to the Caribbean Islands and spent several months chasing Spanish ships and fighting off the coast of Puerto Rico and Cuba. John White didn't like it, but he tried to be patient.

Finally, in August, they set sail for Roanoke. When they got there and anchored off the coast, they saw smoke from a big fire. They thought that it might be a signal from the colonists, so they loaded several men in two boats and headed for the smoke. The captain had been afraid that his ship would run aground in the sand, and he wasn't taking any chances. He dropped the anchor way out in the ocean, and it was so far out that it took them just about all day to row to the beach. Then they had to hike into the forest to find where the smoke was coming from. When they got there, they didn't find anything but a fire. By then it was too late to do anything but row back to the ship to spend the night.

The next day the captain moved the ship in closer to the beach, and then the men loaded up the two boats and rowed in toward Roanoke Island. But a storm blew up and the water got rough in a hurry. The first boat made it to land, but the second boat flipped over and out of the eleven men aboard, only four of them made it. The other seven drowned. After the storm died down, they went looking for their drowned friends, and they brought the ones they could find up and laid them out on the beach for burial. By this time the men were so shook up that they didn't really want to row across the sound to Roanoke Island. John White begged and pleaded, and the captain finally had to give them a direct order to get in the boats. So finally they rowed across the sound and landed on the island after dark. They just sat in the boats all night and blew a bugle and sang songs to let the colonists know they were there.

The next day they finally reached the fort on Roanoke Island. It was deserted and grown up in weeds. There was a big post near the gate where somebody had carved the letters CRO. And on a tree out in the yard the word Croatoan had been carved. There was no sign of a fight so they figured that the colonists had left and gone to live with Manteo's people, the Croatoans. John White told them that the code that he had set up with them was to carve where they were going and to carve a cross if they were in danger. He was happy about the fact that there was no cross. The houses had been broken into by the Indians after the colonists had left, and tools and all their belongings were scattered about, laying out in the weeds. John White found his three chests, but they had been broken into, and it had rained in his trunks and his books and his drawings and paints and paper had been ruined. He had some armor that had rusted almost in two.

After the men had rowed back to the ships, there were darks clouds in the sky again. John White wanted to sail down the coast to Cape Hatteras where the Croatoans lived, but the wind blew up and they couldn't. One ship headed for England, but John White's captain agreed to head back down to the Caribbean and swing back by Hatteras on the way home. When the storm came, though, it blew so long and so hard that it blew the ship way out in the Atlantic, so since they were almost halfway back to England, they decided to head on back. So John White had to give up on finding his family and the lost colonists. He hoped that they were safe and happy living with the Indians.

SECRET MARRIAGE

You might ask how the failure of the colony in Roanoke affected our old friend, Walter Raleigh. Well, he lost a lot of money from it, but Old Walter had a lot of irons in the fire, and he didn't let a setback slow him down. The Queen had given several of her supporters land in Ireland that England had captured during the big rebellion over there. She had given Sir Walter a huge estate in Ireland. It was over 42,000 acres. So he went over there to live and to try farming. Some say that he took a strange Indian food named the potatoes that Manteo and Wanchese had given him and taken them over to Ireland to see if they would grow there. They say he was

25

the first person to introduce potatoes to Ireland. I'm not sure I believe it. You can if you want to.

While he was over there in Ireland, he met a famous poet named Edmond Spenser, and they got to be good friends. In fact, he was good friends with a lot of poets and writers and scientists. In fact, he was a pretty good poet himself.

Anyway, when he came back from Ireland, he started secretly dating one of the Queen's maids of honor, and pretty soon they got married. His wife's name was Elizabeth Throckmorton. They had to keep their marriage a secret, though, because the Queen was a jealous woman, and she didn't allow her servants to marry. When she finally heard about it, she raised hell. She had Raleigh and his bride arrested and held in prison up in the Tower of London. When they got out, they had both lost their jobs so they went down to Dorset to live on his estate there.

VOYAGE TO GUIANA

Now, our story might have ended there. They could have lived there in the quiet countryside, and raised their children and lived happily ever after. But after a couple of years, Sir Walter started to grow restless. He was short of money like most of us, and his solution was not to look for a job. Oh, no. His solution was to go look for the lost city of gold in the jungles of Venezuela. Back then, all of the northern coast of South America was known as Guiana. So Sir Walter went to see some people and put together a small fleet of ships and hired some sailors, and they set sail for Guiana. It was February in 1595. The expedition was financed by several of his friends who wanted to get rich, too.

When they got to Guiana, they talked to some Indians and took some Spaniards captive and questioned them. Everybody said the gold mine was in the jungle, up the Orinoco River. So they hired a guide and loaded all their gear into big old flat-bottomed boats and started rowing up the river. They ran across Indian villages all along the way, and they made friends with all the Indians they met, but they never knew when they would meet some that weren't friendly. The climate was hot and sticky, and the food ran out, so they lived on fish and fruit. One time they stopped for a break, and some of the men wanted to go for a swim. They pulled off their clothes, and the first man who jumped in was grabbed and eaten by a big crocodile right there in front of them. You should have seen all the splashing around and all the blood. You could hear the man scream for miles around. The rest of them decided they'd put their clothes back on and just be sweaty.

Raleigh and his men traveled 300 miles up the Orinoco River. He sent scouting parties out all over looking for gold, but they never found any. Finally, it started to rain. It was the monsoon season, and it poured down for days. The river flooded, and the current was running so strong that they couldn't paddle but one direction. Back down stream.

When they got back home to England, the expedition was big news. A lot of people didn't like Sir Walter, and, when he came back all sun-burned and mosquito-bitten and empty-handed, they couldn't have been more delighted.

The next year Queen Elizabeth sent a fleet of ships to attack Spain. She must have gotten over her ill feelings toward Sir Walter because he served as a rear admiral in the attack. The English sailed to the Spanish port of Cadiz, and there was a big naval battle. The English won. Sir Walter Raleigh was wounded, and he was one of the heroes of the battle. After that, the Queen made him Captain of her Guard again, and Governor of Jersey. He served in Parliament until the Queen died in 1603.

JAMES I BECOMES KING

After Queen Elizabeth died, her cousin, James, King of Scotland, became King of Britain. He didn't like Raleigh and Raleigh didn't like him. It wasn't long before Sir Walter's enemies had accused Sir Walter and others of a conspiracy against the King. I don't know if there was anything to it or not. Anyway, there was a trial, and Sir Walter was convicted and sentenced to death. Three days before the execution he was pardoned and sent to the

Tower prison again. His wife and children were allowed to live there with him. It was kind of cramped, but they lived there for the next 13 years.

King James' policy toward Spain was much different than Elizabeth's. He tried hard to maintain the peace. He didn't have the money to fight a war, for one thing. Anyway, they needed the space in the Tower, so James decided he'd free Sir Walter and let him go looking for that gold in Guiana once again. If he found it, England would get most of it. But he made Raleigh promise that he would not attack the Spanish. King James knew that the Spanish wouldn't give up any gold without a fight.

There was a big celebration when Raleigh and his men sailed off for Guiana once again. It didn't take them long to get there, and, sure enough, they hadn't been there but a few days before Raleigh's men got into a fight and killed a bunch of Spaniards. Sir Walter's son was killed in the battle. After that, the men argued, and they finally returned home to England. When they got there, Raleigh was arrested, and there was another trial. He was sentenced to death. His execution was big news, all over England. They took him up on this stage where a big crowd could see the execution. He knelt down and put his head on a block, and this great big executioner with a black hood chopped his head off with a great big axe. Twenty-six years later, King James' son, Charles, would be executed the same way by Oliver Cromwell's men.

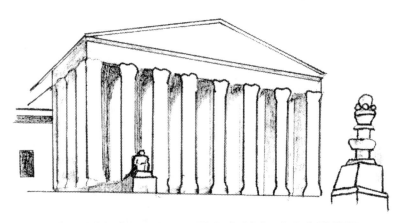

HOW LOUIS BRANDEIS GOT APPOINTED
TO THE SUPREME COURT

Louis Brandeis was appointed to the United States Supreme Court in 1916 by President Woodrow Wilson. He
served on the Supreme Court for 23 years.

There are nine judges on the Supreme Court. Don't ask
me why, but they aren't called judges. They're called justices.
Every time the Supreme Court decides a case, one of the nine
justices writes a report on why the court decided the case the
way they did. The cases are decided by a vote among the nine
justices. The majority wins. Sometimes one of the losers
writes a report on why he or she doesn't agree with the majority. Louis Brandeis became famous for writing about cases
involving the government's right to regulate business. He
believed that the government had a duty to protect people
from all kinds of abuses from the big companies.

THE PROGRESSIVE MOVEMENT

During this time, we're talking about the years between 1900 and about 1920, there started to be a lot of publicity about how big businesses operated in the United States. Almost every day or so there was a story about how companies were cheating their customers and mistreating their workers. As more and more people became aware of what was going on, it made them madder and madder. Some people were trying to change all this. This was called the Progressive Movement, and the changes were called "reforms." The people who were in favor of these reforms were called "progressives."

The progressives were people who read about the abuses of the big companies and wanted to change things to make life more tolerable for ordinary people. Some big companies were making millions and millions of dollars, and they made life miserable for the people who worked for them and they overcharged and cheated the people that bought their products. They also dumped chemicals and dead animals and everything nasty you can think of into the rivers. Not to mention the smoke in the air. Some of these companies were the steel companies, railroads, oil refineries, meat packers, sugar refineries, and tobacco companies. The big companies worked together and made agreements to keep prices high for all the products they sold and to keep the wages they paid workers low. If anybody was trying to organize a union, the big companies hired these big thugs with baseball bats to beat up people at union meetings.

People worked long hours in mills and factories in unsafe conditions for thirty or forty cents a day. In the summer time it would be hot. In the winter there wouldn't be enough heat. It would be real loud with all the machinery running. A man might have his fingers cut off just like that. Or something real heavy might fall on his foot and crush his toes. Young girls worked hard all day at a sewing machine, six days a week in sweaty shirt factories with no heat or ventilation for four or five dollars a week. If you were hurt in a bad accident, you were laid off, and then you went home and maybe you laid in bed for the rest of your life. Then you had to depend on what little wages your wife and children could earn.

Railroads charged farmers outrageous prices to ship their corn and wheat to market, and meat packers ground up rotten meat and mixed it in with the good and sold it to people. They would take it home and cook it and eat it and the whole family would get sick from it.

Some newspaper reporters and writers investigated the factories where people worked and talked to workers and then wrote magazine articles and books about how outrageous conditions were in these jobs. These articles and books stirred the public up and got people upset and complaining about it. These writers became known as the "muckrakers" because they were always digging up dirt on big companies. Of course, muck is more of a mixture of dirt and something else, and the first time these writers were referred to as muckrakers, it wasn't meant as a compliment. But, they liked the name, and they started to use it themselves.

As a result of all this publicity and outrage among people, some progressives and do-gooders would decide to run for the state legislature in their states, or even for the United States Congress. And some of them would win. Then the state legislatures in some states started passing laws to protect workers from having to work in unsanitary and unsafe conditions. They set limits on how old young children had to be before they could work and how many hours a week women could work.

In 1900 Teddy Roosevelt was elected President. Roosevelt was in favor of many of the reforms that the muckrakers were calling for. He tried to stop the big businesses that were working together to keep prices high and wages low. When a big company buys up all the competition and combines them all together, we call this type of organization a monopoly, and today they are illegal. Back then they were called trusts. Roosevelt worked hard to break them up, and he became known as a "trust buster."

That gives you a little background about what mood the country was in during this time. In 1912, Woodrow Wilson was elected president. He was another progressive president who wanted to change things and make people's lives better. And this is where this story begins.

EARLY LIFE

Let me start by telling you a little about Louis Brandeis. He was born in Louisville, Kentucky in 1856. His parents were Jews, and before he was born they had crossed the Atlantic Ocean on a big steamship looking for a better life in America. Louis' father had brought some money with him, and he knew a little about farming, so he went into the grain business. Farmers grew a lot of grain out in Kentucky and the surrounding area, so they went out and visited Louisville. Plus, Louisville was on the Ohio River so they could ship the grain down river on barges. So Mr. Brandeis went into the grain business. He would buy corn and wheat and soybeans from farmers and ship it down to New Orleans and sell it.

Anyhow, the Brandeises hadn't been in Louisville long before little Louis came along. When he was growing up, it was obvious how smart the boy was. So things were going along real good. They had a new baby and they were making good money in the grain business. Then, along came the recession of 1873. Mr. Brandeis lost so much money he had to close down. They decided to move back to Germany where they had family. They went back home to a town named Dresden. Little Louis went to school in Dresden, and I guess he had learned German at home back in Louisville, because he went to school in Germany and he did real good. German schools back then were tough, but he worked hard and made good grades.

A couple of years later the recession was over, and the Brandeis family decided to load up and move back to America and try again. Louis applied to Harvard Law School in Boston, and he was accepted. So he moved to Boston and started classes. He worked hard, and his hard work paid off. When he graduated, he had the highest grades in his class.

After he graduated, he went out to live in St. Louis and practice law so he could be near his parents, but he missed Boston. So the next year he moved back to Boston and opened a law office with one of his old Harvard classmates.

MR. BRANDEIS MAKES ENEMIES

In his first case as a lawyer in Boston, Louis took a railroad company to court and kept them from building a railroad track through the middle of Boston Common. Boston Common is a nice big shady park right in the middle of downtown Boston.

After that, he began to make a reputation for himself all over the country. He was the kind of lawyer that was not afraid to take cases and take large corporations to court to protect the interests of the general public. He went up against the gas company and the insurance industry, and in 1908 he won a case before the United States Supreme Court in Washington, DC. In that case he defended the state of Oregon. The Oregon legislature had made it against the law for women in Oregon to work more than a certain number of hours every week. Big business didn't like that law, so they took the state of Oregon to court. Brandeis won the case and the law stayed on the books.

Next he went up against the New Haven Railroad. The New Haven Railroad had gone around and bought almost all the major railroad and steamship companies in New England, and Louis opposed all these deals. He said they were creating a transportation monopoly.

This time Louis made some very rich and powerful enemies.

He was interfering with some multi-millionaires who wanted to make even more millions. These rich men had friends who owned newspapers. They began to say ugly personal things about Louis in the local newspapers. They brought out that he was a Jew to try to play on people's negative emotions.

That case lasted several years, but in 1913 the court ordered the breakup of the New Haven Railroad monopoly. Almost instantly our Mr. Brandeis was a national figure. People either loved him or hated him. Lawyers from all over the country tried to get him to testify in their cases. These cases were about life insurance, antitrust law, public utilities regulation, labor unions, and giving women the right to vote. Back then only men could vote.

Over the years Brandeis and his partner had built up a nice law practice, and they were making good money. But the way he lived didn't change. He spent his free time reading aloud with his family, riding his horse, and rowing a boat up and down the river. He took his family down to the beach for their vacations.

The wealthy men of the old Boston families did not understand Mr. Brandeis. They thought people with money were supposed to join the country club and the men's clubs and play poker and golf. They hated being beaten in court by a self-righteous lawyer who just didn't fit in. He didn't even like to go to baseball games or football games.

LOUIS BRANDEIS GETS INVOLVED IN THE PRESIDENTIAL ELECTION

When the campaigning started for the presidential election of 1912, Woodrow Wilson, the governor of New Jersey, was running, and Louis Brandeis liked him, and he decided he'd do what he could to help him get elected. He started writing newspaper articles endorsing Woodrow Wilson. He told all the reasons why he thought Wilson would make a good president.

Mr. Wilson read the articles in the newspaper, and he wrote a letter to Mr. Brandeis and asked for his help in the campaign. Wilson owned a big beach house down on the New Jersey shore, and he invited Louis down for a weekend so they could talk and get to know one another. After that, Brandeis spent a lot of time with Wilson. He gave him advice on economic matters and on how to get his message out to the public. In the final weeks of the campaign, Brandeis went on a tour to make speeches for Woodrow Wilson. He traveled all over the New England and New York and the Midwest making speeches. As it turned out, Woodrow Wilson won pretty easily, and he became the thirty-third President of the United States. A lot of people thought that Louis Brandeis' help had made a lot of difference in the election. They expected that Brandeis would be appointed to be the next Attorney General or Secretary of Commerce or maybe some other important post in Wilson's administration.

THE NEW PRESIDENT DISAPPOINTS HIS SUPPORTERS

President Wilson was grateful to Louis for his help, and he wanted to make Louis a member of his cabinet. But the new President's advisors told him that appointing Brandeis to anything would be a big mistake. They said that Brandeis was considered kind of a radical, and some of Wilson's more conservative supporters hated Mr. Brandeis, especially the ones in Boston. They said appointing him would be like poking a stick in their eye. So when the President was picking someone for Attorney General, he picked somebody less controversial. And when he picked a Secretary of Commerce, he skipped over Brandeis again.

This made a lot of people disappointed and angry. You see, there were a lot of people who wanted things to be changed in this country, and they worked hard to try to get people elected to office who were honest and not so greedy and not so willing to help out their rich friends. These people were called the progressives. The progressives felt like they had finally elected a president who was one of them. But now their hero, Woodrow Wilson, was becoming a big disappointment. By not appointing another hero, Louis Brandeis, they felt that Mr. Wilson was caving in to the enemies.

One of Woodrow Wilson's closest advisors was Josephus Daniels. He was the editor and the owner of the Raleigh, North Carolina, newspaper, <u>The News and Observer</u>. Josephus Daniels told people that President Wilson was not happy with having to leave Brandeis off his cabinet, either.

PRESIDENT WILSON ASKS LOUIS FOR HIS HELP

About a year later, President Wilson called Louis Brandeis on the telephone. He said he needed his help again. He said he needed some advice. Mr. Wilson had been working for a long time on creating a government agency that would oversee and regulate the banks all over the country. The bankers and their friends, of course, were against government regulation, and the President was having a hard time getting Congress to pass it. Mr. Wilson asked Brandeis if he would come down to Washington and talk to him about it.

Louis said he'd be glad to. He thought that this was an important issue that would determine how banking was done in this country for years and years. He was right. When he got there, he and some other experts sat down and came up with some ideas. They decided that money should still be issued by the government and not the Federal Reserve Bank. They also thought that the government should keep control of the Federal Reserve Board. Finally they got Congress to pass it, and this is the system we still use today.

The President asked Mr. Brandeis to help out in writing other laws that Congress passed during the early years of the

Wilson administration. They created the Interstate Commerce Commission and the Federal Trade Commission.

When the Federal Trade Commission went into effect, all the progressives celebrated. But pretty soon they were going to be disappointed because the commission was not very effective. A lot of the men President Wilson appointed to the commission were businessmen who didn't want to take action against the big companies when they broke the law. Of course, the Senate has to approve all the president's appointments, so when the President tried to appoint men who were progressives to the Commission, the conservatives in the Senate raised hell and were able to block the nominations.

THE APPOINTMENT

So the President was fed up, and when one of the Supreme Court justices died, he thought about it and finally said, what the hell, and appointed Louis Brandeis to the vacant seat on the United States Supreme Court. On the day the President announced what he was going to do, every newspaper in the country ran it on the front page. All over the country, the progressives celebrated, and the conservative newspapers wrote mean and bitter editorials condemning Wilson and condemning Brandeis.

The President can't just appoint somebody and they get the job. Appointments to the Supreme Court have to be approved by the Senate just like the cabinet positions, and everybody knew that there was a lot of opposition to Mr. Brandeis. He was well known as one of the leading progressives in the country. In fact, some people would call him a radical. And on top of all that, he was a Jew. Back then some people held that against a person. And all the members of the Supreme Court were conservatives, and it had always been that way. So everybody expected a big showdown.

Some of the country's leading newspapers came out against the appointment of Louis Brandeis. Big-time papers like the *New York Sun*, the *New York Times*, the *Wall Street Journal*, and the *Detroit Free Press*.

Some pretty important men came out and made public statements about how President Wilson was making a big mistake. People like former President William Howard Taft, the president of Harvard University. Mr. Taft had been President of the United States before Woodrow Wilson. Also, both the Senators from the state of Massachusetts, Louis' home state came out against him.

The way the system works is like this: the nomination goes to a subcommittee first. They hold hearings and then vote on it. Then it goes to the Senate Judiciary Committee. They hold hearings on it and then vote. Then it goes to the floor of the United States Senate. They debate it, and then they vote on it.

OPPOSITION

The people that were determined to keep Louis Brandeis off the Supreme Court got together and hired them a high-powered lawyer to organize all the opposition. Seven big-name lawyers that had served as presidents of the American Bar Association got together and wrote a letter to the subcommittee. They said Brandeis was not "fit" for the office of Supreme Court Justice. Fifty-five prominent Boston citizens signed a petition that opposed the nomination. The petition said Brandeis was dishonest and untrustworthy.

Of course, they knew he was not dishonest. These are the real reasons they hated him so bad: number one, he was a Harvard Law School graduate, and Harvard Law School graduates are the elite, and the elite are very conservative. Louis just did not fit the mold. He had turned against his own by becoming one of the reformers. Second, he was a very clever lawyer, and he was always coming up with what you might call unorthodox tactics in the middle of a trial. In other words, he had outsmarted a lot of these high-priced Boston lawyers and beat them.

Louis' third offense was that he was not a member of the "in crowd" of Boston society. Number four, he was a Jew. Now, being Jewish was not a big factor, but it was a factor. Back then the majority of Americans were Christian Protestants. Their ancestors had come from England and Scotland and other Protestant counties in Northern Europe, and they kind of looked down on everybody else.

THE PROCESS

Now, Mr. Brandeis' supporters were not just sitting around doing nothing. They got busy and got some important people together to help him win this thing. Louis' law partner back in Boston and his life-long friend said he wanted to do anything he could to help. His name was Edward F. McLennan. He volunteered to move down to Washington to coordinate all the supporters' activities. Another good friend was George W. Anderson, a United States attorney. His job was to help everybody get prepared to testify in the hearings.

There were three Democrats and two Republicans on the subcommittee. The subcommittee called in people to speak for the nomination and others to speak against the nomination. Some people testified that Louis was ruthless and unscrupulous. They went on and on about him. But in the end they couldn't name one thing that he had done wrong. The hearings lasted two or three weeks. When the subcommittee finally voted, the three Democrats voted in favor of the appointment, and the two Republicans voted against it.

Then the confirmation process moved on up to the full Senate Judiciary Committee. Now the center of attention was focused on five Democrats who said they were undecided. There were ten Democrats altogether on the committee, and eight Republicans. Everybody knew the Republicans would all vote against Mr. Brandeis, so the five Democrats who were already on board knew they would need these five undecideds to carry the vote over the eight Republicans. Also, everyone was sure that if the nomination was approved by the Senate Judiciary Committee that the full Senate would pass it pretty easily.

So everything depended on these five undecided Democrats, and each one of them had what he thought was a good reason for voting against Brandeis.

Senator James O'Gorman of New York was in a big ongoing quarrel with President Wilson, and anything the President was in favor of, he was against.

Senator Jim Reed of Missouri wanted to run for president next time, and he didn't want to make too many people mad by voting for a progressive like Louis Brandeis for the Supreme Court.

Senator John K. Shields of Tennessee and Senator Hoke Smith of Georgia were unpredictable. They were from the South, and the southern politicians were always very conservative back then.

Senator Lee Overman of North Carolina was a former president of a railroad, and the railroad executives all considered Brandeis the enemy because he had brought so many court cases against them because of the outrageous rates they charged.

So Louis' friends and supporters knew they had an uphill battle on their hands. The chairman of the Judiciary Committee stalled and delayed committee meetings for over a month. He wanted to give the supporters time to do what they had to do to win.

At the time Harvard had nine law professors. Seven of them sent a strongly worded letter saying what a smart man and good lawyer Louis was. Two of these seven had been Supreme Court Justices themselves. They were Felix Frankfurter and Roscoe Pound. A former president of Harvard sent another letter. President Wilson sent another letter.

WORKING ON THE FIVE UNDECIDED SENATORS

Senator Jim Reed was a tall, lanky fellow from Missouri. Some women might have thought he was handsome, and he probably thought so, too. He knew how to make a good speech, and old Jim wanted to be President real bad. He had fought against every piece of progressive legislation that had ever come before Congress, bills like the one that created the Federal Trade Commission. He had even said some bad things about one of the progressives that were pushing this legislation, a lawyer named Louis Brandeis. But old Jim knew that if he ever wanted to be President, one of the steps he needed to take was to be the next Democratic Party leader.

Remember when I told you about the reporters and writers that wrote about how bad the conditions were for factory workers? And how big companies were selling unsafe products to the public and charging outrageous prices? Well, one place they published their articles was in a magazine called <u>Colliers</u>. The editor of <u>Colliers</u> was one of the country's leading progressives. So, this editor threw a party at his home one night and invited Louis Brandeis and a bunch of his friends and some of the Senators on the Judicial Committee.

Well, Senator Reed decided to go to the party, but he didn't intend to stay long. He would run in and make an appearance and leave. Just like some state representatives do today. But after Senator Reed got there, he met Louis Brandeis, and they struck up a casual conversation, and they ended up talking for over an hour. Then suddenly the Senator jumped up and went looking for his hat and coat. He had suddenly remembered that his wife was outside in the car waiting for him. But when he finally went out that door, he knew, and Louis knew, that he was going to vote in favor of confirmation.

The other member of the Senate Judiciary Committee who attended the party at the editor's home and talked with Louis was Senator Hoke Smith of Georgia. Senator Smith had served eight years as governor of Georgia, and he had been the United States Secretary of the Interior. He was recognized as one of the most powerful members in the Senate. Senator Smith was also a long time friend of Woodrow Wilson. He had helped Wilson get elected in the 1912 election. Senator Smith had introduced Wilson to Josephus Daniels, editor of the Raleigh <u>News and Observer</u>. Josephus Daniels later became Wilson's Secretary of the Navy and one of his closest advisors.

Senator Smith had always been against the rich and powerful men on Wall Street and against the big trusts. In other words
he was for everything that Woodrow Wilson and Louis Brandeis
stood for, and you would think he'd be the first one to vote for
Louis, but Senator Smith refused say how he'd vote. He was from
Georgia and Georgia was a very conservative state, just like it is
now. He knew if he declared himself for Brandeis, all his political enemies back home would have a field day. They would stir
up a lot of racist hatred against him because Brandeis was a Jew.
Smith was planning on running for Senator again, and he knew
something like this could really hurt him down in Georgia.

Several weeks later, one of President Wilson's friends went
to talk to Senator Smith in private. Smith told him that he was
disappointed that he and other Senate leaders were not consulted
before Wilson went and made that nomination. And he said that
the President had not invited him over to the White House in
over three months. But he said he was probably going to vote for
Brandeis, anyway. Then three or four days before the vote, Smith
declared he would vote for the nomination.

Just before President Wilson made his appointment, James
O'Gorman, the Senator from New York City, had announced
that he was going to retire from the Senate. He was not going to
run in the next election. He had voted against his party several
times, and the President had not appointed some of the Senator's
friends to various jobs that he had recommended them for. So he
and President Wilson were not getting along very well.

So the President sent Secretary of the Navy Josephus Dan-
iels and the Assistant Secretary of the Navy, a young fellow from
New York named Franklin D. Roosevelt, to talk with Senator
O'Gorman. It seems that before all these problems came up that
O'Gorman had let it be known that he would like to become a
Federal judge. Daniels and Roosevelt reminded him that if he
voted against Brandeis it was going to be mighty hard for Presi-
dent Wilson to appoint him to anything.

Then something happened. It seems that there was this man
from New York named Jeremiah Lynch, who had come over from

Ireland years before and had stayed in New York and become a naturalized citizen just like so many Irish people had done over the years. Anyhow, it seems that Jeremy Lynch had gone back to Ireland to visit his family and had gotten into some trouble while he was over there. It was Easter and Jeremy had been hanging out with some buddies who were known to be freedom fighters. There had been a big demonstration that turned into a riot and some people had gotten killed. It became known as the Easter Uprising. Jeremiah Lynch was one of the ones arrested by British soldiers. He and all his friends were tried and convicted and sentenced to hang.

Senator O'Gorman went over to the White House to ask President Wilson if he could do anything to save Lynch. Wilson said he'd see what he could do. So Wilson got on the phone to London to the United States ambassador to Great Britain and asked him to see what he could do to save this man. Finally, they were able to work out a deal so that Jeremiah Lynch's sentence was reduced from hanging to ten years in prison. This made Senator O'Gorman a hero in New York. After that, there was no longer any doubt about how the Senator would vote on the Supreme Court nomination.

Senator Lee Slater Overman from Salisbury, North Carolina, was the number two man on the Senate Judiciary Committee after the Chairman. On the day of Wilson's announcement about the Brandeis appointment, reporters were asking everyone what they thought about it, and he had told them that he didn't believe that Brandeis would be approved. He did say, though, that the testimony in all the hearings may change some Senators' minds.

By April Senator Overman still had not said how he would vote. But Josephus Daniels told President Wilson not to worry about it. He said that Senator Overman and he were both from North Carolina, and that they had been friends for a long time. He said Senator Overman never crosses a bridge until he gets to it. He said that Senator Overman had never voted against any nomination of the President yet and he wouldn't this time.

Then, once again, something happened. Mecklenburg

County in North Carolina claims to have been the first government body in the English colonies to declare itself independent from Great Britain. The date was May 20, 1775. So every May 20, Charlotte used to have a big Mecklenburg Declaration of Independence celebration. President Woodrow Wilson had been invited to come down and speak this year, and he had accepted. Then, he felt like everything was falling apart, and World War I was going on over in Europe, and he sent word that he just couldn't take time off and leave Washington.

Well, Josephus Daniels and both North Carolina Senators went to the President and asked him to change his mind. Finally, he said he'd go. They all rode down together on the train.

There is a main railroad line that runs from Washington to Charlotte and on down to Atlanta. Now it so happens that that line runs right smack through Salisbury, North Carolina, the home town of none other than Senator Lee Slater Overman. Well, of course, Overman wanted them to stop in Salisbury on the way down, and he wanted to appear on the platform with the President of the United States and have the President speak to his home town constituents.

President Wilson said he was tired and hoarse and had a lot on his mind, and they didn't have time to stop in Salisbury. Josephus Daniels went in to talk to him again, though, and reminded him that they needed Overman's vote to get Louis Brandeis approved.

Anyway, they stopped in Salisbury and the President appeared on the platform with Senator Overman. Wilson told the crowd that they could be proud of their Senator. He said that the world is at the beginning of a new age, and America will have to play a very great part in that new age. He said there were men who were trying to hold us back. That he and Senator Overman were trying to move the country forward.

From there they went on down to a great celebration in Charlotte. The Governors of North Carolina and South Carolina were there and local congressmen and mayors. The newspaper claimed they had over 100,000 people. Most of them, like today, had never seen a President before. And back then, they didn't have television or radio. When the President came out and spoke, the crowd went wild.

After that, they went on back to Washington, and they knew they didn't have to worry about Senator Overman's vote any more.

The last of the Democratic undecideds on the Judiciary Committee was Senator John K. Shields from Tennessee. He had been real sick and, he had spent most of the time for the past two or three months back at his home in Tennessee. He was an independent-minded man, and he was another Senator who was not getting along very well with the President.

While he was laid up back home, several important men who were against Louis Brandeis came to see Senator Shields. Some of them were good friends who had helped him in his campaign. They were really putting him in a bind.

At the same time, President Wilson's daughter had married a man from Tennessee. His name was William McAdoo. Woodrow Wilson had made Mr. McAdoo his Secretary of the Treasury. So Mr. McAdoo called his friends down in Tennessee and had them go and talk to Senator Shields. When he got back to Washington, Senator Shields was asked to come up to the White House for a talk with the President.

But the Senator still refused to commit himself. He had just become the senior senator from Tennessee, but he knew he would not be able to get anything done for his state or get his friends appointed to offices in the government unless he cooperated with the leaders of the Democratic party. But he would not say how he planned to vote until he actually voted.

Of course, Senator Shields did vote in favor of the nomination. All ten Democrats voted to confirm the nomination. And, as everyone expected, all eight Republicans voted against it.

When President Wilson heard the news, he knew that the nomination would be approved by the full Senate. When it finally came to a vote in the Senate, the vote was forty-seven in favor to twenty-two against, and the nomination was confirmed. All Democratic senators except one had voted in favor of the nominee and all Republicans except three had voted against it.

While the voting was taking place, Louis Brandeis was on a train headed to his home in the little town of Dedham, Massachusetts. He didn't know when they were going to vote. When he got home and his wife opened the door, she had a big grin on her face. Somebody had called from Washington and let her know. She said, "Good evening, Mr. Justice Brandeis," and gave him a big hug.

And Louis Brandeis went on to become one of the Supreme Court's most respected justices.

But President Woodrow Wilson couldn't spend time celebrating his victory. He was dealing with getting the military ready in case we had to go to war. Also, there was a revolution going on in Mexico, and, on top of all that, the presidential election was coming up in November. His opponent was going to be Charles Evans Hughes, who used to be on the Supreme Court, and it looked like it was going to be a tough race.

In spite all of these problems, though, Woodrow Wilson had taken the time to use the power of his office to push the Brandeis nomination through the Senate confirmation process. So it must have been something he believed in pretty strongly.

THE SHORT LIFE OF TITUS,
EMPEROR OF ROME

A note from the grandson:

BRIEF HISTORY OF ROME

Rome began as an humble farming village in south-central Italy around 600 BC. The hamlet prospered and soon became the central market place for the surrounding villages. Four centuries later Rome was a sprawling cosmopolitan city, famous throughout the Mediterranean as a major center for the arts, for learning, and for its engineering and architectural feats. The Mediterranean world also knew Rome to be a formidable military power. By 200 BC, Rome controlled the entire Italian peninsula, and Roman influence and domination continued to spread to territories throughout the region. By 200 AD, the Roman Empire stretched from Spain to Palestine and from England to North Africa.

Rome was ruled by the city's wealthiest families. Male members of these families served in the Senate, and they governed the republic until 44 BC. As Rome grew and extended its trade and its influence around the Mediterranean, so did another major power in the region, a large, thriving city in North Africa called Carthage. Carthage had established trading ports in Sicily, in Corsica, and in Spain, a major source of precious metals. The rivalry between Rome and Carthage led to conflict and two extended wars. The Romans won both, but the price of victory was high.

The first war ended with a truce in 241 BC. The second erupted four years later, and the fighting went on for 35 years. In 218 BC the Carthaginian general Hannibal made a surprise invasion from the north with his famous war elephants. His army swept into Italy to capture several key cities, and he continued to inflict havoc in the Roman homeland for fifteen years. With the defeat of Carthage in 202 BC, however, there was no force in the world that could resist the advance of the Roman armies into all parts of the known world.

In 44 BC, the popular general, Julius Caesar, declared himself Emperor of Rome. Although he was soon assassinated by several jealous senators, this moment transformed Rome from a republic to an empire under imperial rule.

As the empire expanded, the Romans maintained control over conquered lands by bringing law and order and trade and prosperity to all parts of the empire. Soon Roman citizenship was offered to loyal local inhabitants throughout the empire. Consequently, Roman citizens in Spain, Britain, Gaul, and Macedonia became equal in status to citizens in Rome.

The Roman soldiers, in addition to being the most disciplined and most efficient fighting force in the world, were excellent engineers. The Roman highways stretched from southern Spain to the northern coast of Germany, to the Black Sea, to Syria, and across the continent of Africa. Cool mountain water flowed to cities hundreds of miles apart through great aqueducts high in the air. The army constructed walled cities and fortifications wherever they were stationed. Soldiers stationed at faraway posts married local women and remained to raise families and add genetic diversity to the area.

In Roman cities the wealthy enjoyed lives of luxury which included fine wines, jewelry, and palaces with tapestries, monuments, and elaborate ornamental carvings. The great aqueducts supplied water for ornate public baths and for extravagant fountains and indoor plumbing in the homes of the privileged. The Romans built great public temples and forums, victory memorials, amphitheatres, walled cities with great harbors, bridges, and sewer systems. Roman roads, fortifications, archways, and columns remain in place today in many parts of Europe.

Another Roman legacy is a highly refined legal system. The written laws of Rome were respected by all Roman citizens and were uniformly applied throughout the Empire.

From the death of Julius Caesar in 44 BC until Rome was overrun and sacked by the Visigoths in 476 AD, the empire was ruled by a succession of emperors. Some ruled with wisdom and courage and presided over long periods of peace and prosperity. Some expanded the empire and constructed roads, temples, and aqueducts. Others were vile individuals who tortured and murdered political enemies and made major blunders in foreign policy. Some emperors were generals who seized the throne in times of turmoil and civil war. Some were emperor for only a few years or less.

My grandfather's next story is about a Roman emperor named Titus.

TITUS

This is a story about an emperor of the Roman Empire named Titus and his family. Their last name was Flavian, but not many people used their last names back then, so he was known as just plain Titus.

Just about everything I know about Titus came from a biography of Titus written by an American historian named Brian Jones. Mr. Jones wanted a catchy title that would help sell more copies of his book so he named it <u>The Emperor Titus</u>. He did a good job, though, and I enjoyed the book.

It seems like after all these years public opinion on how good an emperor Titus was is still undecided. For example, in his book, Mr. Jones says that an ancient historian named Suetonius described Titus as "the delight and darling of the human race." And Josephus, a Jewish governor who later lived in Rome and became a historian, described the turnout for Titus' victory parade in Rome. He said that out of the entire population of the city of Rome, not a single person stayed home that day. And Tacitus, another Roman historian who lived during Titus' time said Titus was a genius. He said his face "mingled beauty and majesty."

Some of the historians since that time think that maybe Titus was a man of many talents and was a pretty good emperor. But there are plenty more that don't think so. They say that Titus was a mediocre character with a fine reputation but not much real talent for leadership. They think that Titus was like a lot of today's public figures, that he just knew how to say the right thing to manipulate public opinion.

The Jewish historians, of course, don't have anything good to say about Titus. That's because he was the general who burned down their fabulous Temple of Solomon in the middle of downtown Jerusalem during the first Jewish revolt. Mr. Brian Jones, who wrote that book about Titus, says he was a brutal man and vain, and that he had no patience as a general and that he wasted a lot of the empire's money while he was Emperor.

The best sources for learning what really happened in any period of history is from what we call primary sources. Primary sources are people who wrote about events that happened during their lifetimes. Our best source for Titus' story is a book written by a Jewish priest and general named Josephus. Josephus was captured by General Vespasian, Titus' father, and he was forced to ride around with Vespasian and Titus for the rest of the war, and pretty soon Titus and Josephus became best friends. Later on Josephus was hired by Titus and his father to be their public relations person. He could speak several languages, and he must have been a pretty good writer. But you see the problem. Josephus was hired to write good things about Titus and his family, and that's exactly what he did. So we can't believe everything he says, but we do find out a lot of details from him about how history was unfolding at this time. Now, Josephus was a real character with his own unusual story. I'll get more into his story a little later.

JEWISH UPRISING

Sometimes in history ordinary people become famous because a war breaks out or some other catastrophe, and ordinary people happen to be in the right place at the right time and they do what needs to be done. Ulysses S. Grant comes to mind, and Abraham Lincoln, and maybe Harry S. Truman except for his dropping those two atomic bombs on Japanese cities. The same thing happened to Titus and his father and his brother. Their big chance came in 66 AD. It started when the people of Palestine took to the streets and threw rocks at the Roman soldiers. Then it became more serious, and pretty soon gangs of tough Jewish fighters began to roam around and kill Roman soldiers whenever they could. The situation developed into what we might call today a full scale insurgency.

Really, you need to look back 100 years before this to find the roots of this problem, back when Rome was still a republic. One of the most famous generals back then was General Pompey. Well, in about 63 BC I think it was, he led an army into Judea and they just marched in and took over the place. Then, as always, the Romans looked around and found themselves a local official who would work with the Romans, and they appointed him to serve as the local king. The king would be king as long as he did things the way the Roman army wanted him to.

You can imagine how the average Hebrew people in the streets felt about this. They didn't like it. They were angry. Time went by and another generation came along. Then another generation. All the Jews' anger and resentment was passed down from one generation to another. Rome had brought peace and prosperity, but the people didn't like being occupied by Roman soldiers, and they didn't like paying taxes to Rome.

Then this new emperor came along named Gaius. This man was a real lunatic. His nickname was Caligula. Caligula made a lot of arrogant moves that outraged people all over the Empire. And he didn't care. The thing he did in Judea that stirred up the locals was that he ordered his statue to be set up inside the Temple of Solomon in Jerusalem. This was in about 40 AD.

Then along came another new emperor named Claudius, and then, after him, came Nero. Both of these emperors sent some real jewels to be governor of Judea. It seemed like the men they sent either turned out to be crooks or to be completely ineffective, or both. Finally the people of Judea got completely fed up. They gathered in large crowds and shouted insults at the Roman soldiers. Then they started throwing rocks. Then they out and out attacked the soldiers. This was in 66 AD. The local soldiers couldn't handle the situation so they called for help. The Roman governor of Syria next door got his army together and marched over into Judea to put down the rebellion. They thought they would go in there straighten those people out in a couple of days' time. But when they got there, they were in for a surprise.

52

They found out the hard way that it wasn't just a few troublemakers that they were up against. The whole country was up in arms. And the Hebrew people knew how to fight. Before long, the Romans were turned around and sent running back to Syria.

VESPASIAN ON THE MARCH

This was an outrageous, humiliating defeat for Rome. Nobody runs the Roman army out of town, even if they are outnumbered. It was unheard of. And when the news got back to Emperor Nero, you can imagine what his reaction was. He was determined to restore order to the region and to punish the rebels, but the more he thought about it, he decided he had to choose the right man for the job. Nero was afraid to send his best generals out there because they might score so many victories and become so popular they could come back and challenge him for the throne. He was always suspicious that people were cooking up plots behind his back. As it turned out, he was right. Anyway, that's why he chose an older retired general. He was a trusted veteran, too old to have any lofty ambitions. His name was Vespasian. Vespasian's choice for his second-in-command was his young son Titus.

Nero gave Vespasian four legions of soldiers, and as soon as they were ready, they began their march to Judea. That must have been a large army because the Romans had only 30 legions throughout their empire. Anyhow, the Romans marched in and attacked and captured one town after another. In Galilee they surrounded the city of Jotapata. When they captured it, one of the prisoners was a Jewish general named Josephus.

JOSEPHUS

When the Romans found out how important Josephus was, they brought him before General Vespasian. After they had talked for a while, Josephus made a prediction. He prophesied that Vespasian would one day become Emperor of Rome. Now, Josephus couldn't have said anything to please Vespasian and his son Titus any more. They decided that Josephus was some kind of genius, and they decided to keep him with them as an interpreter and advisor. Josephus didn't have a choice. He was a prisoner. Titus kept Josephus at his side throughout the rest of the war. So Josephus was there on the spot when Titus and his men captured Jerusalem.

I'm going to stop here and tell you a little about Josephus. He was born in 37 AD. He came from a family of rich aristocrats, and some of them were priests. His father wanted Josephus to be a priest so he sent him to Jerusalem to study Jewish law at the training school for rabbis. According to Josephus' book about his life, he was so smart and such a scholar that priests and elders of the city consulted with him on interpretations of the law when he was only fourteen years old. Now, really, you can't blame a man for writing good things about himself. Wait until I write the story of my life.

Now, at that time there were three denominations of Judaism, you might say. They were the Pharisees, the Sadducees, and the Essenes. Josephus spent time studying with all three of them. Finally, when he was sixteen, he went to live in the desert with a hermit to meditate and make a decision about which of these three sects he should join. Three years later he made his decision. When he returned to Jerusalem, he joined the Pharisees. The Pharisees were kind of the in between party. They believed in reform, and changes didn't bother them so much, but they were faithful to Jewish law and respected Jewish traditions. They didn't like being ruled by the Romans, but they had just about settled on accepting things the way they were. At least, more than either of the other parties had. Josephus came from a rich family of aristocrats, and they almost always joined the Sadducees. Nobody knows why he made the choice he did.

At age twenty-six, Josephus had become a priest, and he made a trip to Rome. Some of his fellow priests had gone there and gotten into some trouble. Their trial was coming up, and Josephus was sent to see what he could do to help. His ship wrecked and sank on his way to Rome, and, after swimming all night, he and his fellow travelers were picked up by another ship.

When he finally got to Rome, Josephus looked up a famous Jewish actor and asked for his help in getting some fellow Jews out of prison. It turns out that this actor was Nero and his wife's favorite actor. Apparently Nero and his wife loved plays, and they made it a point to get to know the performers. Anyway, Josephus went to the Jewish actor and the Jewish actor went to Nero's wife to ask for her help. Not only did she help get the priests off, but she sent the Jewish actor gifts. This is all according to Josephus' book.

When Josephus returned to Palestine in the spring of 66 AD, he had heard that the Jews were talking about an armed revolt against Rome. He knew the outcome would be a disaster, and he tried to talk them out of going to war with Rome. But the leaders of the revolt were hot-headed and hard-headed, and they wouldn't listen.

Josephus was appointed Governor of Galilee, the Jewish territory located north of Judea. He went up there and immediately began to train his men to defend Galilean cities against Roman invaders. It was a gigantic task, but he did it in spite of the fact that he didn't think they really stood a chance against the Romans.

Josephus turned out to be right. When Vespasian and his army arrived in Galilee, Josephus' men fled in all directions at first sight of that huge Roman army. Josephus escaped and hid out in the city of Jotapata, but Vespasian's men surrounded the walls of the city and began an assault. The battle was mean and bloody, and a lot of soldiers were killed. It lasted forty-seven days, but finally the Romans broke though the gate and took control. Josephus was one of the prisoners they captured.

When Josephus was brought before Vespasian, he told the general that he had a vision and he wanted to make a prophecy. Vespasian thought maybe this guy was some kind of nut, but they were always looking for a laugh. Soldiering was a hard life, especially so far from home, so they were always looking for entertainment. So the old general asked Josephus what his vision was, and Josephus surprised everybody. He prophesied that Vespasian and his son would both become Caesar, master of all the land and all the sea and all the human race. As far as I know, Vespasian had never even thought about being Emperor of Rome, but after that, he decided that he kind of liked Josephus. And from that time on Josephus was part of Titus and Vespasian's inner circle. And when Titus went back to Rome, Josephus went with him to live there and write books for the rest of his life.

WHO'S THE EMPEROR THIS WEEK?

Now let's get back to our story. General Vespasian and his army marched through Galilee and Judea, capturing city after city. He was a pretty good general. A general has a lot to think about, you know. A big army takes a long time to get packed up and get moving every day. Somebody's got to make sure all those men have something to eat and all those horses are fed. There's a lot of equipment that has to be hauled around. Guards are posted, scouts are sent out to report back about what's ahead. Spies have to be hired. And all the plans for the attacks on each city have to be made. There was a lot to think about.

Some people probably thought the only reason Titus had gotten to be a general at such a young age was because he was Vespasian's son. Well, Titus turned out to be a pretty good military commander. The Romans conquered thirteen cities during a two-year period, and Titus' men captured five of them.

While all this was happening way out in Palestine, things were falling apart in Rome. First of all, the Emperor Nero was a selfish, mean-spirited man, and he had always been paranoid. He always suspected others were trying to kill him and take over. Now he was ordering the arrest of some of Rome's leading senators and military commanders and having them executed. Suddenly, all the leading citizens were afraid for their lives. A lot of them packed their families up and left Rome and went into hiding. Finally Nero's own personal bodyguards, the praetorian guard, got fed up with him one night, and they stabbed him to death.

When that happened, this old general, who was a governor over in Spain, decided he would head back to Rome and make his move and try to become Emperor. His name was Galba. When Galba and his army arrived in Rome not too long after Nero's assassination, they arrested the captain of the praetorian guard. His title was Praetorian Prefect, and this was an important position. It seems that this captain of the guard was trying to maneuver himself into becoming Emperor himself. Anyway, Galba's men arrested him and executed him along with any soldiers that happened to be out on the streets in that vicinity when he was captured.

A few days later old Galba was proclaimed Emperor, and people celebrated all over the Roman Empire. They were glad to be rid of Nero. But then Galba got off to a bad start. First, he had a lot of senate leaders and military commanders who were loyal to Nero arrested and executed without any kind of trial. These executions took place not only in Rome but up in Germany and down in Africa. Then he managed to make the soldiers mad all over the empire. For one thing, he made discipline more strict, and for another, he refused to give them a bonus that they had been promised.

On top of all this he surprised everybody by picking somebody to be his heir to the throne, and not that many people had heard of the man. This was really a mistake. Galba's right-hand man for many years had been this guy named Otho, and this really upset Otho. In fact, he was so upset that he and his friends sneaked into the palace one night and stabbed Galba to death and then went into where this unknown heir was asleep and killed him. Otho was then declared Emperor.

All this chaos set off a chain reaction. Now this general up in Britain who had been a friend of General Galba was upset. His name was General Vitellius. General Vitellius decided he would gather his legions in Britain and Germany together and march on Rome and attack Otho's army. Now that was a real mess. You had Roman soldiers fighting Roman soldiers in a civil war that lasted several months.

When the news reached Judea about all these dramatic changes in the political situation in Rome, General Vespasian decided to put a halt to his military operations until he got orders from the new Emperor, Galba. He sent his son Titus to Rome to see if Galba had any new instructions for him and his army. There may or may not have been a rumor floating around that Galba was planning to adopt Titus and make him heir to the throne. It doesn't really matter one way or the other, though, because Galba was murdered before Titus could get to Rome. When Titus heard this, he didn't know what to do so he turned around and went back to Judea.

VESPASIAN BECOMES EMPEROR

When Galba was assassinated, Otho became Emperor, and then Otho was assassinated, and the word was that Vitellius was to be the new Emperor. About this time all the generals in the eastern part of the empire had started to encourage Vespasian to lead them in a march on Rome to restore order and to claim the throne for himself.

So Vespasion and his friends sat down and came up with a plan. Their plan called for a man named Mucianus to lead the main part of Vespasian's army against Vitellius. Mucianus was currently serving as governor of Syria, and he was one of Vespasian's top supporters. Vespasian must have thought he was a pretty good general, too. The other part of the plan was for Vespasian himself to take some men and travel to Egypt to meet with the Roman generals there and make sure that they would support him. That way he would have control of the grain supply. That was important, because Italy got a lot of its grain from Egypt, and Vespasian knew if he had control of the grain supply he would have the upper hand. And Titus' job was to stay in Judea and take over the fight against the rebels there.

When Vespasian had made his decision to make his move, he remembered that Josephus had prophesied that Vespasian would become Emperor. He decided to set Josephus free. They had a big ceremony, and Josephus' chains were cut in two with an axe in front of everybody. That was the way they demonstrated that Josephus was a free man with a full pardon.

Meanwhile, when General Mucianus reached Rome with that big army, Vespasian was declared Emperor. Mucianus took control of the empire until the new Emperor arrived from Egypt. Now, Vespasian had another son, younger than Titus. His name was Domitian. Domitian lived in Rome, and he was there to help General Mucianus. They did a pretty good job of restoring peace to Rome, and Vespasian got there ten months later from Egypt to take the throne. They had a big parade and celebration, and people were hoping things would get back to normal. They were sick and tired of all the fighting and bloodshed.

Vespasian turned out to be a pretty good emperor. To show you how things were starting to change in the empire, Vespasian had not started out as a member of the senatorial class. His father had been a tax collector. They were members of the equestrian class, the next step down. Vespasian had risen up through the army. He had a lot of common sense and he was a hard worker. He listened to people. He was Emperor for ten years whereas all three of the previous three emperors put together had lasted less than a year.

Meanwhile, Titus and Josephus were back in Palestine still trying to put down the revolt there. But the whole uprising was about to come to a head because the Romans were marching on Jerusalem. Now, Jerusalem was a pretty big city, and it was not going to be easy to capture. Titus knew the Jews would put up a terrible fight to defend their sacred city, but he knew if he could take control of Jerusalem, the rebellion would be over.

The city was surrounded by three high walls in some places, or either one wall on top of a cliff. The outer wall had ninety towers, thirty feet high and thirty feet thick. The middle wall had fourteen towers, and the inner wall had forty. During the attack, the Jewish rebels would all go up on the walls throwing spears and rocks and shooting arrows.

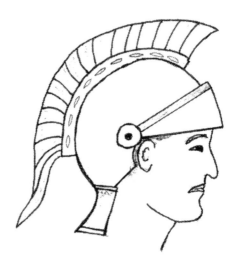

When Titus first got to Jerusalem, he and a few of his men rode up to take a look at the wall. Suddenly a big band of rebels came riding out a gate in a surprise attack. Titus and a few of his men got cut off from the main body. He didn't have on his a helmet and armor. So, do you know what he did? He charged. When a hole opened up, he made it back to his army. Titus was pretty tough.

THE SIEGE

Anyway, the Romans surrounded Jerusalem and settled in for a long battle. It took them five months to take the city. Most cities back then had a wall around them, so it was nothing new for the Romans to surround and capture a city by a process called a siege. The Roman soldiers were very disciplined, and they took things step by step. They would cut off the water supply to the city if they could, and they built wooden towers higher than the walls. The Roman archers could sit up there in those towers and shoot arrows down into the city. They had these giant catapults that they used to sling these tremendous stones into the city. And they had a gigantic battering ram that swung like a playground swing that swings sideways to knock holes in the gate and break it apart. When they rolled the battering ram up to the gate, it was covered with a shelter made out of animal skins or metal plates because the people in the cities always tried to pour hot tar on the soldiers at the battering ram. Sometimes the Romans built bridges on their wooden towers that could be lowered down to connect them to the top of the wall. Sometimes they dug tunnels under the walls.

The people in the city defended the city by pouring hot tar over the wall or throwing stones or shooting arrows. Another tactic was to ride out suddenly and try to set fire to the towers or the catapults and ride back in before the Roman cavalry could get there. Sometimes the Romans dug canals around part of the city to prevent the enemy from riding their horses out to attack.

Titus used these same tactics to capture Jerusalem. His men used a gigantic battering ram to smash in the gates, and they had these big catapults that hurled a fifty-pound stone into the city from four hundred yards away. They built three towers seventy-five feet high, and archers sat inside the towers and shot arrows at the rebels up on the walls day and night.

When they finally fought their way into the city Josephus asked Titus if he could try to talk to the rebels. He wanted to try to get them to surrender before the whole city was burned down and the beautiful old Temple of Solomon was destroyed. But one group of rebels wouldn't listen. The Romans had to keep fighting until every last rebel fighter in that bunch was dead. By that time the city was on fire, and the Romans went ahead and let the temple and most of the city burn down. Thousands and thousands of people had died in the fighting, and thousands had died of starvation during the five month siege. No wonder the Jews hated Titus.

Titus had some of the captives executed, but he kept a lot of them for slaves. Some of them would be sent to work in the mines, and some of them would be trained to fight as gladiators.

Titus spent that winter in Judea, and he rewarded his men for being so loyal and for doing a good job by having a celebration. Part of the celebration was what they called the games. The games were when large crowds of spectators sat in a stadium and watched gladiators fight wild animals or fight each other. One of the ancient writers said that Titus set up a celebration for his brother's birthday that lasted several days, and around 2500 prisoners died before it was over.

In all, he spent seven months marching around the country with 10,000 troops as a show of force in case anybody else wanted to try to start up the revolt again.

Finally, Titus packed up and started on his long march back to Rome. The year was 71 AD. He had been gone five years. When he finally got to Rome, the whole city turned out to give him a hero's welcome. Vespasian had settled in to his new position as the most powerful man in the world, and he ordered a spectacular celebration for his son. During the festivities Vespasian announced that Titus was the "Proconsular Imperium" of Rome which meant that Titus was designated to be the next Emperor. Vespasian did this so that Titus would automatically become emperor when Vespasian died, and there wouldn't be another civil war among the generals. He wanted to establish a dynasty and bring stability and peace and prosperity back to Rome. Titus was also put in charge of the praetorian guard, the Emperor's bodyguards. This was unusual because this job was ordinarily held by a Roman knight, a member of the equestrian class. I guess the old man wanted someone there that he knew was loyal. Anyway, Titus took over a lot of the responsibilities of the Emperor. He made laws and read speeches in the Senate in his father's name.

Josephus had come back to Rome with Titus. He lived there in the royal palace like a member of the family. Vespaian rewarded him for his service by making him a Roman Citizen and giving him a pension.

Now that Titus is about to be the next Emperor, this is probably a good time to stop and let me tell a little about his background and what kind of person he was.

EARLY LIFE OF TITUS

Titus was born in 41 AD. His father, Vespasian, was an army officer, and he was away from home a lot. The Emperor at this time was Claudius, and Claudius needed a playmate for his son, Britannicus, so he let Titus live in the palace and receive the same education Britannicus did.

The boys got to be real close friends. Every day these tutors would come in, and Titus and Britannicus both grew up to be highly educated young gentlemen. They learned to sing and play the harp, and they wrote plays in Greek and poems in Latin and in Greek. The boys had lessons in language composition, and they studied the great epic poems of Homer and Virgil and the great philosophical questions of Greek and Roman literature. Also, they learned rhetoric. That was to prepare them to be able to stand up and argue on the floor of the senate. In the United States Senate today, they still use rhetoric. Some people call it rhetorical b.s.

Anyway, when he was growing up, Titus was a good boy. His teachers all liked him, and he caught on real quick to everything they taught him.

Titus and Britannicus took military training under the Praetorian Prefect, which, if you remember, is the name for the captain of the Emperor's guards. Titus caught on to military training real quick, too. He loved riding horses and fighting with swords. He grew up to be big and strong, and he went off to serve three years in the army in Britain and in Germany. Before long he earned a reputation as a hard-nosed fighter who wasn't afraid of anything.

In 64 Titus decided to come back to Rome to pursue a career in politics. He decided to get married, and he married a pretty girl who was the daughter of a soldier who had once been the Prefect of the Praetorian Guards. This was a little unusual because Titus was a member of the most elite, the highest class of people in the Roman Empire. They were called the senatorial class. His wife was the daughter of a man who was in the class one step below the senators. They were called the equestrian class.

You see, back then the lines between classes was pretty clear. Only a few per cent of the people were at the top. They were the wealthy landowners who held the high government offices. They lived in luxury in grand palaces and big country homes they called villas, and their children automatically became members of their class. They couldn't be taken to court or arrested and tried as criminals.

The next level was members of the equestrian order. This was where Titus' wife came from. One traditional career of the equestrians was the military service. They became the middle commanders. Certain top jobs in the government were reserved for members of the equestrian order. Some of them were Viceroy of Egypt, Commander of the Fire Service for the city of Rome, and Praetorian Prefect, which was the commander of the Emperor's palace guard. Some of them served as administrators in the government, and some were bankers, merchants, and some were large farmers.

The rest of the people in Rome and the Roman Empire, which, really, was most people, were the free men, the freedmen, and the slaves. The freedmen were people who had been slaves who had been set free. A lot of these people were enemy soldiers or foreigners who had been captured in war. Once they were set free they became Roman citizens like everyone else. Now, I don't know what they called females who were free. Free women and freedwomen, I guess.

As I said, the lines between classes were pretty strict, but once in a while there was some mobility. A few top officials of the equestrian class who did a good job and who knew the Emperor or other important people were promoted to the senatorial status. This began to happen more and more as the empire grew and the senators weren't having male babies fast enough. And some free men who had talent and worked hard and became wealthy became members of the equestrian class. Vespasian himself came from the equestrian order and moved up to a top general in the senatorial class.

Anyway, Titus' equestrian wife soon died, and he married a senator's daughter. This marriage did not last, though. The girl's family got into trouble with Nero, the new Emperor, and Titus' family decided that he needed to divorce her. Titus didn't feel that he had much of a choice.

Then Emperor Nero decided to send Vespasian to Judea to put down the revolt, and the old general picked Titus to be his second in command. This appointment made Titus one of the youngest officers to get a command as high-ranking as this that anyone could remember. Mr. Jones, the guy who wrote the book about Titus, said he thought Nero approved the appointment because Titus had divorced that young lady, and Nero considered that an act of loyalty.

Anyhow, Titus proved that he could be a good leader. His men liked him because he looked after them and because he didn't mind mixing with them and talking to them as they marched. When they charged the enemy, Titus was out front. One story says that he once killed twelve enemy soldiers with twelve arrows.

Another story tells you a little bit about Titus' ability to use diplomacy. When Vespasian was sent to Judea, he was operating out of Syria, the country next door. When Syria's governor retired, a new one was appointed, and the new governor made his way out from Rome to take his new job, proud as could be. He was a young hot-shot named Mucianus. Well, Mucianus and Vespasian couldn't get along at all. Vespasian was old and tough and wasn't too hung up on being an upper class Roman this far from home. Mucianus was young, and he was highly educated and wealthy, and he believed in following those army regulations to the letter. So Titus became kind of a mediator. And pretty soon he had Musianus and Vespasian working together pretty closely. Later on it was Mucianus that Vespasian trusted to march on Rome and take over the throne for him. And when Vespasian became Emperor, Mucianus became one of his top administrators.

TITUS FALLS IN LOVE

When you are telling a story, remember, nobody wants to sit and listen to a boring story. And the best way to make a story boring is to make it too long or not to include a little gossip about worldly women and their influence on world events. Women are much more interesting than men. This story of Titus does include a very colorful woman, and her name was Julia Berenice. Remember, now, young Mr. Titus had divorced his second wife not long before he left for Judea, and he had not been out there long before he met this beautiful Jewish princess, and he fell head-over-heels in love with her.

Julia was thirteen years older than Titus, and she had been married three times. She was the sister of the Jewish king, Agrippa II. Agrippa was loyal to the Romans, and he joined forces with Vespasian to fight against the rebels. You see, none of these political situations is simple. They never are. Anyway, that's how our young general met Julia. From then on, he spent as much time as he could with her.

When Titus left to go back to Rome in 71, he left her in Judea until he could pave the way with his father and send for her. She had just about given up hope of coming to Rome to live when, one day in the year 75, she got a message from Titus in Rome. It didn't take her long to pack up and set out on that long trip to Rome. When she got there she moved into the palace with Titus, and they lived there together, happily, for the next four years.

Then, in the year 79, Vespasian's men uncovered a plot against the Emperor. Titus didn't mess around. He found out who was behind the plot, and he took swift action. Several important people were executed. One of them was a man named Caecina. It seems that Caecina received an invitation to a big feast at the palace. When he got there, Titus had a little surprise for him. Titus ordered his men to take care of him. They cut his throat and cut him up into little pieces. I guess Titus was sending a message not to mess with his daddy. When they checked the

dead man's pockets, they found a letter from another important man in Rome. When word got to him, he went ahead
and committed suicide. It so happened that this guy was one
of the main ones that was talking bad about Titus having a
Jewish mistress living at the palace.

All these executions made enemies of the friends of those
that died and started making people feel nervous. Vespasian
asked Titus to send Julia back to Judea until things calmed
down. Titus hated to part with her, but, once again, he didn't
feel like he had a choice.

A lot happened in 79. First, Titus had to send Julia back
home. Then Vespasian died and Titus became Emperor. Then
Mount Vesuvius erupted in southern Italy. Vesuvius was a
volcano that had never erupted before since people first moved
there as far as we know. Anyway, the hot lava flowed down
and completely covered the city of Pompeii, another city
named Herculaneum, and several more. This lava trapped
people and preserved them and their belongings and kept
them from decaying. Then, hundreds of years later, archae-
ologists started digging into these ruins, and a lot of what we
know about how the Romans lived was discovered in these
cities that were buried in this hot lava.

EMPEROR TITUS

Titus may have been a good ruler like his daddy, or he
may have turned out to be another nervous, selfish, despicable
emperor like his little brother, Domitian, was later on. We'll
never know because Titus was Emperor for only two years. He
died at the young age of forty-two. Before he died Titus had
brought Julia Berenice back to Rome, but she caused so much
of an uproar in the Senate that he had to send her away again.

Some people said Titus was poisoned by his brother, but

I was reading a book by a guy named Michael Grant who has written several books about Rome, and he doubts that Domitian had anything to do with Titus' death. Anyway, Domitian ruled Rome for the next fifteen years. But that is another story. This one was about Titus, and he died, so the story is over.

STORIES ABOUT PERSIA

A note from the grandson:

The long and colorful history of Persia, now Iran, began with the bands of primitive tribesmen who arrived from the north and formed a nation that by 500 BC had conquered the entire Near East and built an empire that stretched from Turkey to western India. Territories occupied by Persia included land known today as Pakistan, Afghanistan, Turkmenistan, Uzbekistan, Armenia, Iraq, Turkey, Syria, Jordan, Lebanon, Israel, and Egypt.

Some of the conquered peoples were from highly advanced civilizations, more advanced than the Persians themselves. The pragmatic Persians were quick to adopt what they considered the best from each. Leaving the governments and local customs of occupied countries intact, they provided a peaceful environment for people from diverse regions to travel and learn, to trade and prosper, and to further develop their own civilizations. Consequently, the Persian Empire consisted of a widely diverse collection of peoples and customs, from the highly civilized and economically developed Egyptians and Babylonians to the berry-pickers and herdsmen of the north.

Merchants traveled safely on a well-guarded and well-maintained system of roads that extended throughout the empire. An efficient postal system tied the empire together with the use of dedicated civil servants that traveled by horse, mule, or camel.

The Persian emperors and their families enjoyed fabulous personal wealth and lived lives of luxury in outlandishly grand palaces. They wielded absolute power over the people of all the captured territories, but they did not rule with intimidation and repression as has been the pattern of more recent autocrats. The empire was divided into twenty provinces which they called "satrapies." Persians were appointed to govern each satrapy, but the locals served as administrators, and the people were left alone to pursue their livelihoods as they had before the Persians arrived.

Persian leaders were skillful military commanders, and the huge Persian army was well trained and disciplined. Foreigners subject to Persian rule were welcomed into the Persian army. As a result, the large standing army included units of cavalry and infantry from all over the empire.

The Persian Empire was Greece's major rival during the height of Greek civilization. Wars between the Greeks and the Persians began in 499 BC and lasted for twenty years.

In 330 BC the centuries-old Persian Empire came to an end, brought down by the invading armies of Alexander the Great.

My grandfather had several stories to tell about Persia.

STORIES ABOUT PERSIA

A big part of what we know about Persia comes from a Greek historian named Herodotus. He wrote about the wars that took place before he was born between the Greeks and the Persians. Now, old Herodotus is considered the first true historian because he was the first writer to try to get the facts straight. Most of the writers back then were hired by a king, and they wrote stories that made the king look good. Some writers wrote to show that their people were good and their enemies were evil. But not old Herodotus. He was writing just to leave a record of what happened.

But still, he couldn't speak any language but Greek, and a lot of his stories are based on tales that have been told and retold and translated, and if these translators are like me, each one probably added his own touches to the stories. So I take it all with a grain of salt.

Anyway, some time ago, these tribes of nomads drove their herds down from the mountains south of Russia and settled in the land we now call Iran. Some of these settlers were called Medes, some were called Persians, and there were a couple of others, but they all spoke the same language. They probably moved because they got tired of the Assyrians raiding their homes and stealing their livestock and their women. I don't know which they hated worse.

Anyway, the tribes hadn't lived too long in the new land before this man who was a Mede was appointed to the office of judge for his small village. He was a wise man, and pretty soon he started to make a name for himself. People from villages all around started hearing about what a wise and fair judge he was and that he couldn't be bribed. So people for miles around started bringing their grievances and disputes to him. The man's name was Deioces.

Well, one day Deioses decided to retire and just kind of relax and tend to his garden. I guess he was just burned out.

Anyway, they couldn't find a good and wise person to replace him, so the crime rate shot up. So eventually each of the Median villages all sent representatives to a conference to decide what to do to bring peace to the area. What they decided was that they needed somebody to take charge and bring law and order back to the land. They decided what they needed was a king. And guess who they thought of to offer the job to. Yep, it was old Deioces.

THE NEW KING OF THE MEDES

The first thing the new king did was to set up a system of taxes. And the Medes must have made good money farming and ranching because it was not long before he had collected enough money to build a big palace high on a hill surrounded by walls to protect himself and his treasury. The story actually says the palace was surrounded by seven walls and each had its own color. The inner wall was supposed to be plated gold and the one outside that with silver.

Now, I don't know if I believe all that. I think somebody got to telling this story and they got carried away. Most cities back then had two sets of walls. That makes more sense. But I do believe that this guy started feeling the need to isolate himself from the public. There must have been some rough characters running around back then. Anyway, he had a hand-picked palace guard, and he stayed in away from all the rest of his subjects. Most of his communications with people, including the legal cases that he heard, were in writing. He set up a network of spies throughout his kingdom so he could nip any plots against him in the bud.

The kingdom consisted of six Median tribes. Deioces ruled over these tribes for fifty-three years. When he died, his son, Phraortes, became king. Phraortes wanted a bigger kingdom, so he attacked his neighbors, the Persians, and they came under his rule. Then he took his army off to the west and attacked the people that had ruled the Medes many years before, the Assyrians. I don't know how many times he tried, but he never did defeat the Assyrians. His reign lasted twenty-two years.

When Phraortes died, his son, Cyaxeres, became king. Cyaxeres was a heck of a military leader. He took his army and captured one territory after another. Before you knew it, he had moved the boundaries of the Median Empire as far west as what we call central Turkey. Something happened back home, though, while he was out fighting the Assyrians. This army of people from up north called the Scythians came sweeping in from up north and took over the Medes home territory. When Cyaxeres came back home, the Scythians held his land and his people captive. He agreed to accept their rule. They ruled the Medes for a number of years.

HOW CYAXERES FREED THE MEDES FROM SCYTHIAN RULE

The way Cyaxeres got rid of the Scythians was by throwing a big banquet for their top generals. Then, when they all got drunk and passed out, his men came in with swords and knives and murdered them. Then, I guess without any leaders to tell the Scythian soldiers what to do, the Medians were able to run them out of their territory pretty easily.

Now that Cyaxeres was finally free from the Scythians, he turned around and invaded Assyria again. The Assyrians had a great empire that had ruled the area for three hundred years. But now all their neighbors were tired of being ruled by them and harassed by them. The Medes' biggest ally against the Assyrians was the Chaldeans. The Chaldeans were the people who lived in what we now call Iraq. Their capital was the famous city of Babylon.

Anyway, this time the Assyrians were defeated, and after their victory, there was a big celebration, and then the Medes and Babylonians made a formal alliance. Back then whenever two powerful countries made an alliance, they tried to seal the deal with the marriage of somebody from the ruling families. Cyaxares gave his daughter, Amytis, a pretty young thing, to be married to Nebuchadnezzar, the great king of Babylonia. I don't know how she felt about it, but, anyway, she didn't have any choice. But there is a story that Nebuchadnezzar built the famous hanging gardens of Babylon to resemble the natural mountain gardens of Media so Amytis wouldn't be homesick.

MANDANE'S VINE

After a reign of forty years, Cyaxeres died and his son, Astyages became king.

Bear with me, now. I'm getting to the good part.

One night King Astyages had a dream. He dreamed that his daughter, Mandane, made water in such an enormous quantity that all of Asia was flooded. The king went to the Median priests to interpret his dream. They were called the Magi. They told him that the dream meant that one day Mandane's offspring would rule Asia.

Astyages didn't like that. He felt threatened by it. So he came up with a plan to ensure that his grandsons would never challenge him for his throne. He arranged a marriage for his daughter with a Persian. He considered Persians to be kind of second class citizens, and he didn't believe that a man who was half Persian could ever be considered good enough to rule the Medes.

Anyway, they had the wedding and the daughter went off to live with her Persian husband. Then King Astyages had another dream. He dreamed that a vine growing from Mandane's vagina covered all of Asia. The king called in the Magi for an interpretation. They told him the dream meant the same as the first one, that the daughter's offspring would rule all of Asia.

The king went home and thought about it, and that night

74

he decided that when his daughter had a baby he would have the baby killed.

Before long, sure enough, Mandane got pregnant. Nine months later the baby came, and it was a boy. Soon the king sent his soldiers around to take the baby. The mother screamed and cried and the father tried to fight the soldiers, but there were too many of them, and they were too big and strong.

The soldiers took the baby back to the palace, and King Astyages secretly called for one of his most trusted nobles, a man named Harpagus. Harpagus had always been one of the king's most loyal supporters. The king had shared a lot of secrets with him. He handed the baby to Harpagus and ordered him to take the child out to the country and dispose of him.

Now, Harpagus was a hardened soldier, but he was a good man. He thought long and hard about killing a defenseless child. Finally he decided he couldn't disobey his king. So he called in one of his shepherds and instructed him to take the child out to the pasture and lay him on the ground and leave him overnight to freeze to death.

SPACO TO THE RESCUE

Now the storyteller is asking us to swallow a big coincidence. I don't really like coincidences, but here it is. It seems that the shepherd's wife, a woman named Spaco, had just given birth to a baby who was born dead. She was heart-broken. So guess what. The shepherd took this live baby home and asked his wife if she wanted him. As you would expect, Spaco was overjoyed. She had plenty of milk, so she and her husband decided to keep the boy and to lay their own dead baby out in the pasture.

The couple named their new baby Cyrus, and Cyrus grew up to become the great leader and founder of the Persian Empire. The Persian legend of Cyrus says that he was found and raised by wild dogs. You see how stories get embellished as they are repeated over the years. The fact that Cyrus was nursed by his adopted mother, Spaco, and that *spaco* is the Median word for "bitch," may have had something to do with how that story got started.

Anyway, when Cyrus was ten years old, King Astyages and his guards were out riding around the kingdom, taking care of business, and they just happened to ride through Cyrus' village. It was summer time, and little Cyrus happened to be out playing a game with his buddies. The game was called "kings". Cyrus was playing the part of a king, and he was having the boys who acted as his servants to whip another boy for disobeying his "king".

Astyages stopped his horse and looked at the boy. He looked familiar to him. He called the boy over and talked to him. Finally he realized that the boy had to be his own grandson. He had the boy brought to the palace. He called in the Magi and told them the story. The Magi talked about it and finally decided how to advise King Astyages. They told him that he didn't need to do anything to the boy because Cyrus was no longer a threat. They said the prophecy in his dreams had been fulfilled. It had been satisfied by the boy's role in the game.

Well, the king was relieved. He sent the boy down to Persia to live with his true mother, Mandane, and her Persian husband. The king was still angry, though, with his trusted general, Harpagus, for not carrying out his orders ten years ago. Now, this will show you just how mean a man Astyages was. He decided to take Harpagus' thirteen-year-old son from him. Then he had his servants butcher the boy, cook him, and serve the meat to his father for supper. You can imagine how that made Harpagus feel. But he was able to hold his anger until years later when he was able to pay the king back. This is how he did it:

PAYBACK

When Cyrus grew up, he became the leader of the Persians, and he led an army in a revolt to overthrow King Astyages and the Medes who ruled over the Persians. Well, guess who the commanding general of the Median army was. You guessed it. Old Harpagus. This was his chance to pay the king back for cooking his son. The old general surrendered his entire army to Cyrus without a fight.

Astyages was furious. He went out and raised another army. He took old men and young boys and whoever he could find to march and carry a sword. When he marched them into battle, though, it wasn't much of a fight. Cyrus and his men won easily, and Cyrus became the first king of the Persian empire. The year was 558 BC.

THE CAMELS SAVE THE DAY

But Cyrus didn't just sit back after he put the Persians on top with himself as their king. Pretty soon he was on the road again at the head of his army.

Next door in the western end of what we call Turkey was the home of the Lydian empire. Their king was a man you might have heard of before. His name was Croesus. Whenever you hear someone talking about a person who is very rich, they say he is rich as Croesus.

Anyway, Croesus thought he might just take over some territory while the Medes and Persians were fighting, but Cyrus didn't waste any time. He soon had an army in the field to do battle with Croesus. The two fought a tremendous battle down to a draw. Both armies withdrew to regroup. Normally, wars weren't fought in the winter back then, and since winter was coming on, Croesus headed on back home to sit out the cold weather, thinking he'd return to finish the fight in the spring.

However, this guy Cyrus didn't play by the book. He surprised everybody and he and his army followed Croesus to Croesus' capital, Sardis, and caught him with his pants down. Another battle was fought outside Sardis.

Everybody knew that the Lydians had a large cavalry made up of tough, well-trained troops mounted on fast horses. But Cyrus had another surprise to overcome this obstacle. He had brought along a bunch of camels. When the time came for the cavalries to charge one another, Cyrus had the camels brought out. The sight and smell of the camels spooked and scattered the Lydian horses, and the Persians won the battle, captured Sardis, and captured King Croesus.

Cyrus ordered that Croesus and fourteen of his men to be executed by fire. While the men were being tied to the stakes and the sticks were being brought in and laid at their feet, Cyrus and Croesus talked to one another through an interpreter, and Cyrus started thinking to himself that he kinda liked this guy. He suddenly changed his mind and decided to spare him. But by this time the fire was out of control, and, just as the flames blazed up and surrounded the prisoners, a big downpour of rain put out the fire. Cyrus had Croesus' chains removed, and the Lydian king soon became a member of the Persian king's inner circle of advisors.

By now Cyrus had an appetite for conquering new lands to add to his empire. The object of his next campaign was the great city of Babylon. By now his army was so huge that when they marched, it stretched out for miles, miles wide and miles long. When they stopped to make camp for the night, some of the soldiers had probably pitched their tents, eaten supper, and gone to bed, and the ones in the back end were still marching. Anyway, the Babylonians knew Cyrus was coming days before he got there, and they prepared themselves for an extended siege by stocking enough food and supplies to last several years. Then they raised all the drawbridges, locked all the gates, waited up on the walls with their bows and arrows, rocks, and boiling oil.

The siege was a normal everyday part of warfare back then. Every city was surrounded by walls to keep out the enemies. When they attacked, you rounded up all your people, moved them inside the walls, locked everything down, and waited for the attackers and hoped they would get tired of trying to get in and would go away. The attackers would surround the city, and then they could try to bust the gate in using a big log for a battering ram or they could build some ladders and try to climb up to the top of the wall, or they could just wait until the people inside starved to death.

But Cyrus once again had a trick up his sleeve to break the siege. It seems that Babylon had been built right on top of the

Euphrates River, and the river ran under the walls and provided water for the city. Well, Cyrus had his men dig a canal from the river to a lake that turned the main flow of the river into the lake. So when the water stopped flowing into Babylon, guess what that created where the river bed went under the walls. That's right, a great big gaping hole. And guess who sneaked right into the city from both ends to surprise the Babylonian soldiers. So after a short battle, the Persians took control of the city. And that is how the Babylonian Empire became part of the Persian Empire.

HOW CYRUS DIED

Cyrus' next campaign was against the Massagetae in the territory east of the Caspian Sea. This is the area up north of Iran. Today we call it Turkmenistan and Uzbekistan. I don't know why Cyrus would want it, but he did. Anyway, he first tried to conquer this land the easy way. He offered to marry the queen of the Massagetae. Her name was Tomyris. She turned him down flat. Now you can imagine how Cyrus reacted to her rejection. Word got around, and his whole army knew about it. So Cyrus marched his army across the river into Massagetae territory. The Massagetae army was camped a few miles away.

Remember old King Croesus, who used to be the richest man on earth? Well, now he was one of Cyrus' top advisors, and he had an idea.

Once they had their army across the river, they set up their big colorful tents and prepared an enormous banquet of food and wine. The Persians were famous for their skills at cooking up spicy foods and serving fine wines at fancy parties and banquets. So they did it up right, and they rounded the army up and marched a few miles down the river. The only people left behind to guard the tents with all that food and wine were some servants.

Now, the Massagetae must not have been too smart because when they surrounded the Persian tents and rushed in to surprise them, they slaughtered the Persian servants and sat down to enjoy that fine Persian feast. They ate so much and drank so much that they passed out. The Persian scouts were watching from behind the trees, and when the time was right the Persian army swooped in and killed or captured the entire Massagetae force, which amounted to one-third of the Massagetae army. The Queen's son, Spargapises, was the leader of the defeated troops. He was captured, and he was just as drunk as any of his men. When he sobered up, he was humiliated. He begged Cyrus to release him and give him a sword so he could commit suicide. Cyrus did not want to stand in a young man's way from doing the right thing, so he had somebody hand him a sword, and young Spargapises did himself in right there in front of everybody.

When the Queen heard about the humiliation and death of her baby boy, you can just imagine what her reaction was. She must have been one hell of a woman because she flew into such a rage that she went out and led the rest of her army herself in a furious assault on the Persian army. The battle was ferocious. Both sides suffered heavy casualties, and Cyrus was killed. Tomyris had somebody to take Cyrus' head and peel the skin off of it and make a balloon out of it. Then she filled it up with blood. Don't ask me why. Cyrus had ruled for twenty-nine years.

HOW CAMBYSES CONQUERED EGYPT

Cambyses, son of Cyrus, was the next king of the Persian Empire. His ambition was to add Egypt to the empire. He was looking for a good excuse to invade Egypt. So he came up with an idea. He decided to ask the Egyptian king, a man named Amasis, for the hand of his daughter in marriage.

This put Amasis in a bind. He knew that Cambyses would not marry the girl. If he sent her to Peria, she would become Cambyses' concubine. But how could he refuse the King of the Persian Empire without provoking him? You see, old Amasis was not a dummy. He decided to send a substitute. The girl he sent to be Cambyses' bride was the daughter of the king of Egypt before Amasis.

Well, when the substitute arrived in Persia, it wasn't long before she told Cambyses that she was not the real McCoy. To Cambyses, that was good news. It gave him all the provocation he needed to invade Egypt. He started gathering all his armies together, and they made preparations for a major military campaign.

A Greek soldier in the Persian army named Phanes had been a mercenary and served several years in the Egyptian army. Phanes' captain found out about him and told his general, and soon Cambyses heard about him. Cambyses called Phanes in and made him the official guide for the Egyptian campaign. So Phanes, the Greek, led the Persian army through the desert to attack Egypt.

By the time the Persians arrived in Egypt, though, old Amasis had died and had been replaced by his son Psammenitus. Psammenitus lined up in the field with his army to defend his kingdom.

Before the battle began, the Greek mercenary soldiers who were fighting on the side of the Egyptians demonstrated how they felt about traitors. They knew that Phanes, one of their own, was helping the Persians. Now, for some reason, Phanes' two sons were still in Egypt. Don't ask me why. Maybe their mom was an Egyptian. I don't know. Anyway, the Greek soldiers brought the two boys out to the battlefield and paraded them around in full view of both armies. Then they cut the boys' throats and caught their blood in a big pot and mixed it with wine. Then the Greek soldiers drank it right there on the battlefield.

This made the Persian soldiers so mad that they charged and completely wiped out the Egyptian army. Then they marched right down to Memphis, the real Memphis, and took control of the Egyptian government.

DISASTROUS MARCH ON ETHIOPIA

Next Cambyses made plans to launch military campaigns against Carthage, Ethiopia, and Ammon. Ammon was a country that today we call Syria. In case you don't know where all these places are, I'll give you a little lesson in geography. First of all,

Egypt was a strip of land on the African coast along where the Nile River empties into the Mediterranean Sea and then the land on both sides of the Nile on up into Africa. Maybe I should say down into Africa, because the Nile is one of the few rivers I know of that flows from south to north. Anyway, the whole economy of Egypt was based on farmers irrigating their crops from the Nile. The rest is desert. And Ethiopia was and still is located upstream from Egypt, or, in other words, south of Egypt.

Ammon, or Syria, is located north of Egypt and east of the Mediterranean Sea, kind of to the north and east of Israel.

Carthage was a large city on the north coast of Africa to the west of Egypt and kind of across the Mediterranean from Italy.

So you see, the conquest bug must have really bit Cambyses bad because he was talking about attacking in three different directions at once.

Well, here's what happened. The attack of Carthage did not take place because the Phoenicians refused to transport Persian soldiers to attack Carthage. It seems that the Phoenicians and the Carthaginians were the same race of people and their languages were very similar. Cambyses did not insist because the Phoenicians were good allies and because he depended on them to transport his troops and supplies to where they needed to go around the Mediterranean. Back then Phoenician ships sailed from one end of the Mediterranean to the other trading and hauling passengers and grain and olive oil and metals or whatever people wanted to ship.

In the meantime Cambyses sent spies down to Ethiopia to contact the Ethiopian king and to gather intelligence about the land and the people down there. He would use this information to plan his invasion. The spies came back and said the Ethiopians were extremely tall and strong and claimed to live to be one hundred and twenty years old. The Ethiopian king sent Cambyses a bow and sent word that the Persians had better not invade Ethiopia until they had an army of men who could draw back the bow. When the spies told Cambyses what the Ethiopian king had said, he was so mad that he immediately jumped up and ordered a march on Ethiopia. This was unusual, because he usually sat down and planned a campaign very carefully. This time he acted in haste.

After his army had marched all the way upstream to the city of Thebes, which is three or four hundred miles from Memphis, Cambyses stopped and let his men rest for a day or two. Then he did something that turned out to be real stupid. What he did was he sent a detachment of fifty thousand of his best soldiers across the desert with orders to attack the Ammonites. Then he continued with his main force marching hard as they could toward Ethiopia. Before they reached their destination, though, as you probably already have guessed, their food gave out, and they ate whatever they could find to stay alive. First they ate their horses and pack mules and camels and any kind of grass or weeds or tree leaves they could find. Then they began to starve to death. And, I'm not sure I believe all this, but the story is that they began to roll dice and whoever lost was cut up and eaten.

Finally, Cambyses gave up the campaign and marched his army back to Memphis. The army that returned to Memphis was a lot smaller than the one that had left there several months ago. And the fifty thousand men that he had sent from Thebes across the desert to attack the Ammonites were never heard from again.

THE WRONG SMERDIS

One night when Cambyses was still in Egypt, he had a dream just like his old Median grandfather had years before. He dreamed that a messenger told him that Smerdis sat on the throne of Persia and his head touched the sky. When he woke up, the dream had him all shook up. He thought about it all day. He knew it was just a dream, but it bothered him because he had a brother named Smerdis back home in Persia. He thought about it a long time. It kept bothering him. Finally, he decided to send a secret message back to his man in charge back in Persia. His name was Prexaspes. He asked Prexaspes to hire somebody to murder Cambyses' brother, Smerdis.

83

Back in Persia, Prexaspes got the message, and he couldn't believe it. He couldn't sleep all night long. He didn't want to go through with this. He liked Smerdis. And, as far as he knew, Smerdis had always been loyal to his brother. But he didn't have a choice because the King's orders were the King's orders. So he contacted some lowlifes who loved to murder people and who could keep their mouths shut. They caught Smerdis out on the street one night and killed him.

Anyway, some time after the heinous deed was done, while Cambyses was still in Egypt, somebody did move into the palace and take over the throne of Persia. It was two Median brothers. They were Median priests, which, if you remember, were called Magi. One of the brothers was named Smerdis.

When Cambyses heard that an imposter named Smerdis was on the Persian throne, it made him sick. He knew that he had murdered his brother needlessly. His dream had been a warning of the Mede named Smerdis. When the king realized this, he was so mad at himself and at the Medes that he ran and jumped on his horse like a madman and somehow cut his leg on his own sword. The cut got infected, and he died few weeks later. His reign had lasted seven years, and there were no sons and his only brother was dead, so there was no one to inherit the throne.

DEATH TO THE MAGI

Back home in Persia, the two Magi, Smerdis and his brother, continued to rule Persia. Smerdis pretended to be the dead king's brother, and they hid out in the palace and handled all the government affairs through their servants. They made all their subjects happy by declaring that nobody had to pay any taxes for years.

This went on for several months. Finally some of the nobles started to get suspicious. One of the nobles had a daughter who was one of the king's wives. She lived in the palace. Somebody reminded the nobles that there had been a Magus named Smerdis who had had his ears cut off years before by King Cyrus. So this wife of the king snuck in while Smerdis was asleep to check and

84

feel for his ears. He didn't have any. So she told her daddy, and he told all the other six nobles, so they all knew the truth.

The seven nobles had a secret meeting to decide what to do. Everybody had his own ideas about what action they should take. Some wanted to take action right away, but some wanted to wait a while and see what happened. So they sat and argued and didn't take any action because the one thing they agreed on was that whatever they did, they needed to be in agreement and act together.

Meanwhile, something happened that changed everything. Remember Prexaspes, the King's servant that had Cambyses' brother murdered? Well, old Prexaspes felt so guilty that he climbed up on this tower and made a public confession of what he had done. He told the crowd that the Medes were imposters. Then he jumped off the tower and everybody scrambled back to give him a place to hit the ground.

When the seven nobles heard the news about Prexaspes, that was all they needed. They jumped on their horses and took off toward the palace. When they got there, the palace guards knew what was coming, so they stood aside and let the nobles in. There was a big sword fight in the king's chambers, and the two Magi and their personal bodyguards were all killed, and two of the seven nobles were wounded.

The nobles cut off the heads of the two Magi and ran out on the street to show them off to the crowd outside. The crowd got so stirred up and mad about the way they had been fooled that they went on a killing spree. They ran though the city looking for Magi, and they grabbed and slaughtered every one they could find.

HORSING AROUND

After things had settled down, the seven nobles met to form a new government. They could think of three possible forms government. They were a democratic government, an oligarchy, and a monarchy. They sat around in a circle and talked about the advantages and disadvantages of each one.

One of the nobles spoke against a monarchy. He said that

whenever somebody got to be king, he always started throwing his weight around. He said kings were human and human nature is weak. He said that kings abuse tradition and refuse to obey their own laws. He said they force whatever women they want to become their concubines, and they put men to death without trial. He said he thought the state should be ruled by magistrates who are responsible to the people, and all people should be equal under the law.

Another noble was opposed to monarchy, but he was also opposed to democracy. He agreed that they didn't need a king because kings always abuse their power just like the first noble said. But he was afraid of being ruled by the people. He said the people could be abusive, too. Ordinary people were ignorant, irresponsible, and violent, he said. He wanted the empire to be ruled by a number of Persia's best men. This is called an oligarchy.

A third noble, a man named Darius, said he was against oligarchy and against democracy. He said what they needed was a new king. He was afraid that members of the oligarchy would disagree and fight, and pretty soon they'd have bloodshed and civil war. And democracy, he said, was just as bad. Elected officials took bribes, and he was afraid the people would divide themselves up into little groups and try to make laws favorable to their little group. He said a strong ruler is admired by the people because he breaks up these little groups and opposes corruption and does what's right for all the people. Freedom could best be preserved by the rule of the best man with absolute power, he said.

They talked about it some more, and finally they made a decision. They decided on choosing a new king, but only under certain conditions. They said that one of them should be king and that the other six and their families should get special treatment from the king. They made an agreement that any of those six nobles could always be able to enter the palace unannounced whenever they wanted to unless the king was in bed with a woman. And that the king should choose his wives only from among the seven families.

To choose a new king from among themselves, they decided

that they would all get up early, before the sun came up, and go out to the stable together. Each one would take his horse out and mount him just before the sun came up. The first man whose horse neighed after the sun was up would be king.

Darius was real lucky, because he had a groom that handled all his horses that was real smart. The groom stayed up all night getting Darius' horse ready. What he did was to find a mare that happened to be in heat and tie her outside the stable where they would be coming out the next morning. Then he led Darius' horse round and round and round that mare and got Darius' horse and the mare real excited. Then he let Darius' horse mount the mare.

The next morning Darius brought his horse out with all the other six men and their horses, and they went to the same spot where the mare had been the night before. Darius' horse pranced around and sniffed and snorted and neighed and lightning flashed and thunder clapped and everybody agreed that Darius was the new king of Persia.

The Persian Empire reached its greatest glory under the new king Darius. The empire lasted more than two centuries.

More notes from the grandson:

Herodotus, the ancient historian, visited Persia and wrote down many of the Persian customs. Here are a few of them:

The Persians worshipped the sun, moon, earth, fire, water, and winds. They built no temples, statues, or altars but worshipped the heavens from the mountain tops. Prayers were for the well-being of the king and the community; prayers for personal blessings were not allowed.

Persian birthdays were important events, and each birthday called for an elaborate feast. The meal was served in several courses, and a large quantity of wine was consumed. Vomiting and urinating in public were not allowed, however. Important decisions were made once drunk and again sober.

Persians greeted their equals with a kiss on the lips and those slightly superior with a kiss on the cheek. Men of inferior rank prostrated themselves before Persian nobles.

Persians considered themselves superior to all other people, and each young man was trained to ride, to use a bow, and to speak the truth. Each man had several wives, and the manliness of each was judged by his skill as a soldier and the number of sons he had.

Boys were kept from their fathers until the age of five to spare the fathers from the grief of the death of an infant son.

Persians did not borrow money; they considered indebtedness a disgrace second only to lying.

Rivers were sacred to them; washing hands, urinating, and spitting in the river were forbidden.

THE EFFECTS OF STALIN'S PURGES ON
THE SOVIET PEOPLE

A note from the grandson:

During the 19th century, the industrial revolution transformed the cities of Europe and the United States into centers for manufacturing. The promise of jobs in the factories
attracted thousands of people from the countryside and
produced major population shifts to overcrowded, unsanitary cities. The factories turned out products to be shipped
to consumers, domestic and foreign.

Men, women, and children worked long hours in the factories for low wages. The nature of the machinery employed

in the manufacturing process in many cases required rapid and repetitive movement by the workers. Tragic accidents were frequent. Reporters and social scientists criticized industrialists for their exploitation of the poor and uneducated people who flocked to the cities in search of a means to survive. One of the most famous critics was a German philosopher named Karl Marx. Marx believed that the nature of capitalism created a natural conflict between the industrialists and the workers. Since the workers were the producers of the goods and services for society, Marx believed they should control the land and capital and natural resources. He and others who agreed with him called for a world-wide revolution to create a classless society in which the people controlled production and worked to help everyone reach a higher standard of living.

Marx's revolution took place in only one of Europe's industrialized nations, however, and this single revolution took place thirty-seven years after his death. This nation was Russia, the poorest and least industrialized of the western powers.

TSARIST RUSSIA

For generations Russia had been ruled by an emperor, which they called a tsar (ZAR). The tsar had absolute power. In the first half of the 19th century, 90 percent of the Russians lived and worked on farms. By law the agricultural workers, or serfs, as they were called, were tied to the land they worked and to the owners of the land in a slave-like social relationship. The tsar and the wealthy landowners who supported him resisted any change or reform in the system.

Then, in 1856, the new Tsar, Alexander II, was shaken when the Russian army was easily defeated by France and Great Britain in the Crimean War. He realized that Russia had not kept up with the rest of Europe, and that he must allow industry and some modernization to take place if Russia was to remain a world power.

The Tsar and his advisors soon took action and initiated policies designed to bring the industrial revolution to Russia. Government subsidies stimulated a rapid increase in railroad construction, and the railroads soon brought manufacturing to both Moscow and St. Petersburg. By 1900, Russia was one of the world's leading producers of steel and a major exporter of petroleum.

The Russian people, however, remained underpaid, poorly nourished, and deeply resentful of the Tsar and his government. In 1905, hundreds of protestors were shot down in the streets of St. Petersburg. A wide-spread protest strike persisted, however, and the Tsar finally agreed to an election of a representative legislature, which was called the Duma. After the elections, however, the Tsar was not happy with the makeup of the new body. He decided to dissolve the Duma and rewrite the law so that landowners were assured of a majority of seats in the next election.

WORLD WAR I

In 1914 the nations of Europe plunged into a full-scale war, and the threat of a German invasion united the Russian people. Once more they sang patriotic songs and pledged their allegiance to the Tsar, and the Duma appropriated funding for the war. This Tsar, Nicholas II, proved to be an inept wartime leader. He had not prepared adequately for war, and weapons and ammunition shortages led to the heavy losses suffered by the army in 1915 and 1916.

In March, 1917, food shortages caused riots in the streets, and the riots spread from city to city. Then, in an historic moment, the Duma removed the Tsar from the throne and established a provisional government. The new government's declaration that equality under the law was extended to all citizens as was freedom of religion, of speech, and of assembly brought rejoicing to the crowds in the streets.

A few weeks later the German government provided the radical Russian Marxist, Vladimir Lenin, and his followers with transportation back to Russia. Lenin had spent the previous 17 years in exile in Germany and other European countries. The Germans hoped that he would disrupt the new Russian government. He did not disappoint them.

After his arrival in Russia, Lenin traveled about the country calling for an end to Russia's involvement in the war and for a redistribution of the land to the peasants. In November, 1917, he and his followers, who were known as the Bolsheviks, took control of the government. The serfs swept across Russia, taking control of the land, including large estates belonging to the church, and dividing it among themselves. Workers took control of the factories, and the government took over the banks. Lenin signed a treaty with Germany, giving up all Russia's western territories in order to end the war.

When the elections were held, however, the Bolsheviks won only one-fourth of the seats in the new Constituent Assembly. The Assembly met only one day. On the second day the Bolshevik army permanently disbanded the new Assembly. Lenin's power was now absolute.

Many Russians was outraged. A coalition of opposition forces banded together to form an army and make plans to take back control of the country. Russia was a country torn apart by social upheaval after decades of deprivation under the Tsar, and the civil war brought more misery to the Russian people. The ugly protracted conflict between the Red Army of the Bolsheviks and the coalition of opposing forces known as the White Army ended with a victory for Lenin and the Bolsheviks in 1920.

Lenin moved quickly to consolidate his power by eliminating all opposition to his rule. He created a secret police force that arrested and mercilessly executed anyone who expressed any form of opposition. The promise brought by the revolution had turned to despair as the Communist Party took control of all private property, of the press, and of all economic and social aspects of the lives of the citizens. The Russian people would be ruled by this totalitarian government for the next 70 years. My grandfather's next story describes the horrors of life in Russia under Stalin's rule.

RUSSIA UNDER COMMUNIST RULE

The Russian Revolution took place right in the middle of World War I, and right away the Russians made a truce with Germany so they could drop out of the war. Then the Russians began to fight among themselves to see which group would rule. A lot of the people had died in World War I, and a lot more died when a civil war broke out. It lasted for two years. During all this fighting a lot more people lost their homes and everything they had worked all their lives for. Most of them were poor farm workers, though, and they didn't have much to lose anyway.

Well, the Communists won the civil war, and they set up a government that controlled everything, and I mean everything. They took over the factories, and they decided who could have jobs in the factories and what the factories were to make and how much of it to make and where to ship it when they had made it. They took over the banks and all the money in them. They took over the newspapers and told them what stories to print. They even told the book publishers what to put in the history books. If you spoke out against the government, you might be shipped off to a prison camp way up north in Siberia. Or, you might just disappear and never be heard of again.

Now, when the Communists took control of Russia, it was big news all over the world. Most people in places like France, Germany, England, and the United States thought it was a disaster. The Communists in Russia kept calling for the poor people and workers in other countries to rise up and have their own revolutions. The governments in these other countries were afraid this might happen.

You see, Communism is based on socialism, and the socialists believe that factories, banks, railroads, farm land, and utility companies should belong to the people. They believe that every person should have a job that pays enough to take care of the family, and every person should have free health care. They believe that rich people should have to pay real high taxes, and the government should take this money and take care of the poor and the unemployed and old people.

You can see why rich people who owned big businesses all over the world were so afraid of Communism. A lot of them had made all that money by paying low wages and low taxes and overcharging the public for what they sold them. So they made it a point to get the word out about how evil the Communists were.

Another reason people hated Communism was that the Communists didn't believe in any kind of religion. They thought that the church leaders worked with the kings and the dictators to keep poor people pacified. They may not have decent housing or good roads or clean drinking water or enough to eat, but they had God, and He could help them get through this life on earth. They would get their reward after they died.

The Communists didn't like the strong feelings people had about religion. They demanded loyalty to the nation over loyalty to the church. So they outlawed religion altogether. This gave the anti-communists some really good ammunition. Before it was over, the Communist haters were making every Russian out to be a Godless agitator tirelessly working hand-in-hand with Satan himself to spread Communism all over the world.

But this story is not about Communism. It's about Joseph Stalin.

JOSEPH STALIN

After all the fighting was over from the revolution, Russia was in shambles. The rich had lost everything, and now everyone was equal. Everybody was poor and some people were starving to death.

The farms had no crops and the factories weren't running so people didn't have jobs. The Communists were trying to get the country moving again. The leader of the revolution was a man named Lenin. He was a mean man, but he didn't hold a candle to the guy that took over the government after he died.

Lenin died in 1924. This threw the Communist Party into a real mess. Lenin's right-hand man, a guy named Trotsky, wanted to be the new leader. So did another high-up official named Joseph Stalin. Both of them went around trying to get Communist Party leaders to support them. Finally, Joseph Stalin won. And that was a bad day for Russia. Stalin turned out to be one of the cruelest rulers in the history of this world.

THE PURGES

When Joseph Stalin came to power, he didn't waste any time. He got rid of anyone who opposed him or disagreed with him about any of his policies. And I mean he eliminated them.

For example, one of his right-hand men in the party, a man named Bukharin, kept telling Stalin that he didn't think it was the right time for the government to take over all the farm land in the country. So Stalin had Bukharin and his friends removed from office, arrested, and thrown in prison.

Stalin started his purges with the Communist Party and the government. He found out the names of all the people that had supported Trotsky, his opponent. Then, he had them all fired from their jobs and kicked out of the Party.

Next he decided to clean out the secret police. Back then it was called the NKVD. Don't ask me what NKVD stands for. All I know is later on it became the KGB. I don't know what that stands for either. Anyway, after he cleaned out the NKVD, he went to work on the generals and other officers in the army. We call these actions purges.

During the purges millions of people were arrested and accused of treason or some other related trumped-up charges.

Some of these people were deported and sent out of the country. Others were sent to work camps up north in Siberia. Hundreds of thousands of people were arrested and tortured. When they confessed, they were executed. Some of the important officials might be forced to make their confessions in a big public trial, the kind where everybody knew what the verdict would be before it started. Other people disappeared and were never heard from again.

ONE GROUP AT A TIME

Stalin was crazy, but he was smart. He was careful not to terrorize too many people at one time. He started with the Communist Party in 1933. He ended up kicking one third of the members out of the Party, but most Russians were not members of the Communist Party. Most people didn't know about it and didn't care.

The next year he started the purges all over again. Thousands of members of the Communist Party and government officials were arrested. They were charged with conspiracy against the government.

In 1935, Stalin issued some new laws that shifted the target of the purges from the Communist Party. The new target was the general public. One new law made it against the law to own a firearm or any weapons with a blade. Have you ever tried to peel potatoes without a knife? Another law changed the age for the death penalty to twelve years old. And another law extended the death penalty to people who knew about a spy or about someone disloyal to the government and didn't report it. In other words, if your next-door neighbor said something bad about Stalin and you didn't report it and the government found out about it, you could be arrested for not reporting it.

Anyway, in 1937, Stalin surprised everybody by having all the senior officials in the secret police arrested and shot. Many officials committed suicide before they could be arrested. Some of them did it right there in the NKVD building. Sometimes children of the NKVD officials were arrested with their parents.

Some teenagers committed suicide before their parents could be arrested. Over three thousand members of the NKVD were shot in 1937.

When the arrests of the NKVD officials started, everybody realized that not one soul in the whole backward, frozen country was safe from arrest. People were being arrested for being a friend of a friend of some poor jerk who had already been arrested.

Terror spread around the country. Stalin had a quota for each organization and each city. A quota meant that a certain number of people were taken from each office and shot whether they were guilty of anything or not. Stalin knew that his methods would strike fear in the hearts of every Russian citizen, and no one would have the nerve to complain or criticize the government in any way.

And he was right. People learned that they couldn't trust anyone. They were afraid a neighbor or friend would be arrested, because, you see, anyone arrested would be tortured. And then they would make up some lie and accuse their friends and neighbors just to get the torturers to stop. People quit talking to one another.

COPING WITH FEAR

People escaped and survived Stalin's purges in a lot of different ways. Some cut off contact with everybody and just hid out somewhere. If they ran into anybody they knew, they didn't speak to them.

Some people stayed drunk all the time. A lot of people committed suicide. Some people served as spies for the secret police. The problem with that was that if the spy didn't keep on bringing in evidence on people, the spy would become a suspect himself.

Some people moved from city to city to stay ahead of police paperwork. Some of them hid out in the woods and lived off of the land.

Some people showed a lot of imagination. They would get drunk and cause a disturbance and get thrown in jail on purpose.

They might be in jail for six months. While they were there, they wouldn't be arrested for a more serious crime because nobody really knew where they were.

Some high-up officials quit their jobs and went to work as janitors or park attendants where nobody would notice them. Some moved up to Siberia and froze their hindparts off while they worked at some low-paying job up there.

People became very careful about what they said and who they said it to. Anyone could be a spy for the police. Some historians think that maybe one fifth of the people working in office buildings were paid to spy on their co-workers. There's a story about a woman who had a poodle in her home, and she had him trained. Whenever she had guests in her home and their conversation got real low, the little dog would get up and go push the dining room door shut.

ROBBED OF THEIR HUMANITY

For three years Russian citizens laid in their beds, night after night, stricken with fear. There is a story that sometimes there was a knock at the door in the middle of the night, and the next-door neighbor thought it was his door and committed suicide.

In all, more than seven million Russians were arrested, one million were shot, and two million either froze to death, starved to death, or died of pneumonia or some other disease in those labor camps up in Siberia.

The whole nature of the society in Russia changed. People didn't go out any more or invite friends over for supper. They felt guilty because their friends had been arrested and they didn't try to help. Some people had turned in other people so they wouldn't be arrested, and they felt guilty about that.

When the government would hold a big meeting in a big warehouse or theatre to announce a big arrest of some important officials, people would stand up and cheer even when they knew it was all a lie. They were afraid not to. Sometimes it might have been kin folks cheering.

98

Some people made up accusations about other people for their own personal reasons. Wives got rid of sorry husbands that way. Some people got rid of their neighbors that way so they could buy their belongings.

Every person who had been a member of any political party except the Communist Party were on the NKVD's list of suspects. Soldiers who had served in the White army that fought against the Communists in the civil war years before were on the list. People who had traveled to other countries were on the list. Members of the church were on the list. And everybody who knew anyone on the list was a suspect.

Nothing remained the same. Street names changed constantly because the people they were named for were arrested and executed. Sometimes parks had their names removed, and then they weren't renamed. Bank officials changed so fast that they didn't even bother to sign checks any more. In government offices, nameplates outside the doors disappeared.

One time Stalin got real angry at the city of Leningrad so he ordered every fourth citizen of the whole city to be arrested and sent to prison camps in Siberia. So hundreds of citizens of Moscow traveled to Leningrad to buy cheap furniture, carpets, and other furnishings left behind.

THE NEW ELITE

With so many purges going on and so many people in top jobs disappearing, Stalin needed new managers that knew about machinery and construction and how to handle money and how to run an army and a navy. So he started a nation-wide education program and went out and recruited young Communists who would be loyal to Stalin himself.

Before Stalin's time, the managers of farms and factories and government departments were mostly people who had no education. They were people that used to work on a farm before the revolution. They had fought with the Red Army and been rewarded with these jobs because they were loyal. These managers had people working for them who were the experts. They were the engineers, accountants, and consultants, and most of the time they were not members of the Communist Party. They worked under the managers, but they normally made the important decisions.

Now Stalin wanted to educate young Communists and train them to run Russia's economy. And he didn't have to twist any arms. He went around making speeches to recruit young people to attend technical colleges. Your country needs you. Join me and you'll get a good job making plenty of money. Well, they came off the farms and out of the factories and out of the wood-work in droves. In the next five years, a hundred thousand students or more from the working classes had graduated with some kind of technical degree and got a good job with the government.

Meanwhile, Stalin kept up the purges across the nation, and people kept getting arrested and sent off to Siberia or disappearing. This opened more and more slots up for these new eager young graduates. They were completely loyal to Stalin and to the way he operated, and they kept getting promotions and salary increases. They didn't care about politics or what was going on in the world. All they cared about was machines, new technology, industrial development, the latest techniques for administration, and stuff like that. These new managers and engineers were making a lot more money than the ordinary workers, and they didn't seem to care how ordinary folks were making out. It was no wonder that the wider the gulf got between their wages, the harder the feelings were of ordinary workers toward these new managers.

THE COLD WAR

Everybody had to admit, Stalin did build Russia into a world power. At some point, he had begun taking in countries around Russia and adding them to Russia. This new expanded Russia became known as the Soviet Union.

Russia was attacked by Germany during World War II, and

the Russians fought on the side of Britain and the United States and helped them defeat Hitler. After the war was over, Stalin's army marched in and took over almost all the countries in eastern Europe. They took over Poland, Czechoslovakia, Hungary, Bulgaria, Rumania, half of Germany, and some others. Communist governments were set up in each of these.

Do you think this threw a scare into the anti-Communists in this country and elsewhere in the world? You better believe it. Then the Russians learned how to make atomic weapons, and they started to mount them in the nose of these big missiles, and they pointed them at the United States. And for the next thirty-some years, the whole foreign policy of this country was to out-spy the Russians and to build more missiles than the Russians. This was called the Cold War. During this time people all over the world lived in fear that the United States and Russia would fire all their nuclear missiles at each other and destroy the whole planet.

STALIN DISAPPEARS

In 1953, a lot of people in the Russian government were accused of one plot or another, and it looked like there would be another purge. Then one night Stalin and his top aides all disappeared. When everybody realized that he was gone for good, the Communist Party met for several days and finally picked three new leaders. The top man was an ugly, bald-headed fellow named Nikita Khrushchev.

The Cold War went on until 1989. Every night we went to sleep not knowing whether or not somebody would push the wrong button and all those missiles we had pointed at one another would blow up the whole world. There were novels and movies about it. And there were some movies about what life would be like after the war, with all the radiation. Giant lizards and giant insects hunted for the few people that survived. And people hid out from evil gangs that roamed the countryside. Some people in the United States built underground bomb shelters in their back yards and stocked them with cans of food. Some schools practiced what to do in case of nuclear attack. They had the children to crawl under their desks and cover their heads.

Then, in 1989, the Soviet Union collapsed and came apart. One by one, all those nations that had been ruled by the Russians declared their independence. Now we had to look for a new enemy to aim our missiles at.

ALCIBIADES AND THE FALL OF THE ATHENIAN EMPIRE

This story is about a Greek warrior named Alcibiades. Alcibiades lived in Athens, the greatest Greek city-state. He lived there when the Athenian Empire was at the height of its glory. Now, I feel certain that if Alcibiades lived in the United States today, he wouldn't be very popular at all. First, he was rich, and he was a loud-mouth who liked to brag. Second, he liked to stay out late, drinking and raising hell. And third, he had a lot of boy friends. And I don't mean hunting and fishing buddies.

Of course, times were different back then. Women were second-class citizens pretty much, and they weren't allowed to go to school. What did girls need an education for? And they were not to be seen out in public until after they were married. The boys went to school together, played sports together, bathed together in public baths, and trained together and fought together in the army. A little hanky-panky among friends was not unusual at all.

So, there were a lot of good citizens of Athens who despised Alcibiades because he was such a pompous individual and because he enjoyed such a decadent, wide-open life style. But, there were many other people in Athens who admired him because he was such a colorful character. And even his enemies would admit he was a fierce sword fighter and a fearless leader in the battle.

Alcibiades was also a leader in the Assembly. He had become a member of the leadership at a young age because he was such an eloquent public speaker. He was one of those guys who could sell ice skates in the middle of the Sahara desert.

He was also an enthusiastic sports fan who bet a lot of money on all kinds of public games. He entered teams in the chariot races at the Olympics every year, not just one team, but several. In 416 BC, his teams won three of the top four positions. So, you see, he was a big deal in Athens among the sports fans.

GREEK CITY-STATES

I need to pause here and fill you in on some background information about the position of Athens and the Greeks in the world at that time. First of all, there was no country or nation called Greece back then. Each city or town owned a certain amount of territory around it. Each city or town had its own government, and it was independent from the others. These independent cities with their own territories were called city-states. The Greek word for a city-state is "polis."

There were small city-states that were just a city and a little land right around it. They owned maybe 50 square miles of territory. Then there were the big ones that owned hundreds of square miles of land. Some might have owned 500 square miles. Some of the Greek city-states had become busy commercial centers that were where farmers and craftsmen came from miles around to market their olive oil or their pottery or gold jewelry. From the big trading centers, they could have their goods shipped to other cities all around the Mediterranean Sea, which, back then, was just about all the known world. As these big city-states grew, they were able to just absorb the smaller city-states around them. The bigger and richer a city-state became, the bigger army and navy it could afford. Sometimes these big power-house city-states went to neighboring city-states and required them to pay taxes in exchange for protection.

THE SPREAD OF GREEK CULTURE

As the city-states increased in population, some citizens left to look for a new place to live. They would travel to far-off undeveloped locations and settle down to create new city-states. These new city-states became new markets and trading partners for the mother city-state. By the time of Alcibiades, the Greek people had spread from one end of the Mediterranean Sea to the other. They were just like fire ants. Before long, there were Greek cities all around the coast of Turkey and up into the Black sea where Bulgaria and Rumania are located today. They were located along the sunny coastline of France and Spain and along the coast of North Africa, including Egypt. There were Greek cities on the islands out in the Mediterranean like Cyprus, Crete, Sicily, Sardinia, and Corsica.

The Greeks were real smart and very creative. They constructed great temples and palaces and public libraries. Some of them were highly skilled architects, artists, and craftsmen.

Education was very important to the Greeks. They wrote poetry, dramatic plays, and comedies. Some of their plays are still acted out on the stage today. If you ever see one, the thing that stands out is how much people have not changed in all this time. In fact, their philosophers and historians shaped the European people's and American's world view for the next 2,400 years.

The Greeks carried their culture and their language with them wherever they settled. Just like the English did when they settled in America 2000 years later. By the time of Alcibiades, everyone in all the civilized areas of the Mediterranean spoke Greek. Anyone who couldn't speak Greek was called a "barbarian." This word came into the language because the Greeks couldn't understand foreign languages. To the Greeks they sounded like "bar-bar-bar."

The Greeks were also great farmers. Their olives and grapes were traded all around the Mediterranean.

THE MILITARY MIGHT OF ATHENS AND SPARTA

By this time the Greeks' military might was unchallenged by anyone. The problem was, though, that they fought among themselves. They still used chariots with one soldier driving and another soldier bouncing around on the back end shooting arrows at people. But the newest weapon was the phalanx. The phalanx was a group of foot soldiers who marched together in close formation with shields and long spears, and they operated almost like a tank. The foot soldiers were called hoplites. Each hoplite carried a round iron shield, a short sword, and a nine-foot spear. They wore short skirts, iron vests, iron helmets, and iron leggings over their shins. They lined up in rows of eight or sixteen and marched in step into battle.

Some Greek city-states also had a great navy. The warships were called "triremes." They were powered by three rows of men with oars on each side of the ship. Their strategy in battle was to ram enemy ships with the pointed wooden battering rams mounted in front. These sharp points were down below the surface of the water, so if you could swing around and ram your enemy, you wouldn't have to worry about that boatfull any more. Boats don't float too well with a big hole in the side.

WAR WITH PERSIA

The one country that was powerful enough to challenge the Greeks was Persia. Before the time of Alcibiades, the Greeks faced a major threat from the Persian Empire. Around 520 BC the Persians invaded Greek territory and captured all the Greek cities along the coast of what today we call Turkey. They also captured the Greek cities around the Black Sea.

Then thirty years later the Persians invaded the mainland of Greece, but this time they were defeated by the Greek army. The Greeks won because they were using that new war technique called the phalanx. The Persians tried again in 480 BC, and this time they were able to capture Athens. Most of the citizens of Athens evacuated the city when they heard the Persians were coming. They just packed up and lit out and left the city for the Persian army to march right in. But Athens had the most skilled naval commanders in the world, and while their city was being invaded, they were out in the Mediterranean taking out all their anger on the Persian navy. The Greeks almost completely destroyed the Persian fleet. So that put an end to the Persian threat for a while. The two Greek city-states that played the largest part in the victory were Athens and Sparta. After that, these two became the most powerful of all the Greek city-states. Like maybe San Francisco and LA, or Raleigh and Charlotte. Or maybe Dallas and Houston.

ATHENS VS. SPARTA

The Spartans had a reputation for having the toughest, meanest soldiers in all of Greece. All Spartan boys were taken from their mothers at age seven to live in the barracks and train for the army. They slept on benches and marched around barefoot and suffered all types of hardships. This kind of life made them tough. They could get married at age 20, but they were still required to live in the barracks and serve in the army until they were 30. As a result of this harsh life and all that training, the Spartan army was the most powerful fighting force in that part of the world for more than 200 years. The other reason was they had ten years of stress-free marriage.

Now, Athens was as different from Sparta as night and day. The Spartans studied mostly battlefield tactics in school, and they didn't care much for poetry and art. But the boys in Athens studied literature and music and developed an appreciation for fine pieces of art. Athenian pottery was sold all over the known world. The great Greek philosophers like Socrates, Plato, and Aristotle came from Athens.

And while Sparta was ruled by the military, the people of Athens ruled themselves. All decisions in Athens were made by the Assembly, and all male citizens were members of the Assembly. The Athenian legal system allowed any citizen, no matter how poor, to bring legal action against any other citizen, no matter how rich.

After the Persian Wars, Athens was able to free many of the cities around the Aegean Sea from the Persians, and they formed an alliance to protect them from future attacks. Athens was the leader of the alliance and the member cities were all required to pay taxes to Athens for protection. Athens used all this money to build ships. Before long Athens had a powerful navy and a merchant fleet that carried Athenian products from one end of the Mediterranean to the other.

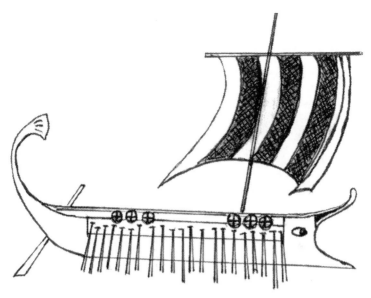

YOUNG ALCIBIADES

Now, let's get back to Alcibiades. Alcibiades came from a wealthy family in Athens. His father was a soldier who was killed in battle when Alcibiades was just a small boy. So he and his brother were sent to live in the household of Pericles. Now, Pericles was the most famous general in Athens and the leading statesman in the Assembly. Alcibiades' mother may have been Pericles' first cousin. Nobody really knows. We just know Pericles raised the two boys like they were his own sons.

Anyway, Alcibiades was a beautiful child and he was very bright. He caught on to things his tutors were trying to teach him real quick. But he was spoiled rotten. I mean he was a self centered, vain, and arrogant little squirt. According to one story, he refused to learn to play the flute when he was a little boy because he didn't like the way his face looked when he blew into it. He said he didn't like the flute because he couldn't talk or sing while he played it. He claimed flutes were for people from Thebes. He was referring to the reputation people from Thebes had for not having much to say. He reminded his teacher that Athena herself had thrown her flute away when she saw her reflection in the water as she played. As a result of Alcibiades' hard-headedness, the flute became less and less popular with the boys in Athens. In fact, it wasn't long before flute playing was eliminated from the curriculum for young men in Athens.

Alcibiades was also very competitive. Once, when he was wrestling, the other boy was about to get the best of Alcibiades, so Alcibiades hauled off and bit the boy. The other boys made fun of him and accused him of biting like a woman. That didn't bother him. He said he was fighting like a lion.

He once ran out into the street and threw himself in front of a loaded wagon. The driver pulled hard on the reins and managed to stop his team of horses just in time. Alcibiades said he and his friends had been playing a game and their dice had bounced into the street and he was trying to get the dice before they got lost in the dust under the horses' hooves.

Just to show you how bold he was and how cunning he was for his age, there is a story about the time Alcibiades wanted to get into Pericles' office to talk to him, but the Pericles' aides wouldn't let him in. They told him that Pericles was busy considering how to "present his accounts to the people." Little Alcibiades thought about it for a minute and said what Pericles should be doing is figuring out "how to avoid presenting accounts to the people."

As Alcibiades grew a little older, he gained a reputation as the life of the party. He liked to gamble, drink wine, and run around with a bunch of boys. There was a rumor that one of his sweethearts was the great philosopher Socrates. They served together in the army.

According to one story, in the middle of a battle, Alcibiades was knocked down and was about to be chopped up into small pieces by some bloodthirsty guys with sharp swords, but his friend Socrates stood over him and saved his life. For that incident, the army awarded Alcibiades a commendation for bravery. That's the kind of guy he was. Everything always seemed to go his way.

Alcibiades was not a coward, though. There's another war

story about a battle when the Athenean soldiers' position had been overrun, and they were in full retreat. Socrates and his compadres were running flat out for the hills with the enemy hot on their rear ends. Alcibiades, on horseback, charged the enemy to give Socrates and the other foot soldiers time to escape. We don't know whether he received another commendation this time, or not.

From what I have read, there is some question about whether or not Alcibiades and Socrates were actually boy friend-boy friend. Some historians think that there's no doubt about it. They think that other historians don't want to tarnish the reputation of Socrates because he was such a great philosopher.

ACIBIADES GETS MARRIED

In another story that shows just how outrageous Alcibiades was, he made a bet with some of his drinking buddies one time. The bet was that he would walk up to this rich and powerful man named Hipponicus out on the street and hit him in the face. Well, he did it. He walked up to Hipponicus, in broad daylight, in a crowd of people, and punched him in the face with his fist. The story spread around the city, and it caused a scandal. The next day Alcibiades had sobered up, so he went to Hipponicus' house and apologized. He offered to let Hipponicus whip him or punish him in any manner he wanted to. Hipponicus was so impressed that he forgave Alcibiades, and they became such good friends that later on Hipponicus gave Alcibiades his daughter, Hipparete, to be his wife. How would you like to be married to a woman named Hipparete?

Anyway, back then it was customary for the bride's father to give the groom a gift of money or property to help get the couple started. It's called a dowry. Hipparete's dowry was ten talents which was a good sum of money during those days. Not too long after the wedding Hipponicus died, and when the first child was born to Hipparete and Alcibiades, Alcibiades went to Hipparete's brother and told him he wanted another ten talents. He claimed it was part of the bargain with her father. As you would expect, the brother was outraged. He finally paid Alcibiades ten talents, but he was so angry that he changed his will and left all his money and property to the city of Athens. That way, Alcibiades couldn't get one more cent.

Do you think that Alcibiades cut out all his carousing after he was married? You are right. He didn't. By this time he was spending time in the company of women, and some of them didn't have such a good reputation even before they started hanging out with him. Back then they were called courtesans. And the whole town knew about it.

Hipparete was furious, as you would expect, and hurt. She felt like everyone was laughing at her. She finally petitioned for a divorce. When her court date came around she went down and appeared before the magistrate. During the hearing, however, she turned around and looked and there was Alcibiades standing in the doorway. He came in and walked over to his wife, smiled at her, picked her up and threw her over his shoulder, and carried her all the way home. On the way, he marched directly through the crowd at the market place. She continued to live with him until she died a short time later. Some people say that this may not have been as scandalous as you might think. There may have been a law on the books that gave husbands a chance to recover their wives in just that way.

ALCIBIADES GOES INTO POLITICS

Alcibiades' wealth, his family background, and his reputation as a courageous warrior made him a natural for a career in politics. His greatest asset, though, was his gift as an orator. He knew just what to say, when to say it, and how to put it. He spoke with a lisp, and he had a habit of pausing in the middle of .... a sentence in .... search of a forgotten word. This made his delivery more powerful. Because he was so articulate and so popular, it wasn't long before he rose to the top, just like cream in a bucket of milk, and became one of the leaders in the Assembly.

But in his private life, Alcibiades continued to stay out late chasing women, drinking, and gambling. And he continued to make a spectacle of himself. Once he walked through the market place dressed in a long, purple robe, which, back then, was the way a woman would dress. He carried a shield made of gold. On the shield was the figure of Eros, god of love. It was almost as if he were trying to make fun of old Greek traditions, and, in the process, he made himself look like a fool. He even had some posts installed on the deck of his ship with hooks on them so he could hang his hammock. He would lay there in his hammock up on deck while they were underway.

A lot of the older and more conservative citizens of Athens were offended by the outrageous behavior of Alcibiades, but the public loved him. Once he was walking down to the Assembly, and he walked through the square and heard them talking about people raising money for the war effort. He stopped and turned around and went back to make a donation. When he handed the man the money, though, but he forgot about his bird, a quail that some people kept and raised and they bet on them. He had it hidden under his cloak. It was pretty common for people to own this type of bird, but they were illegal. Anyway, when he reached for his coin purse, the bird flapped his wings and flew off like he'd been shot out of a cannon. The members of the Assembly roared with laughter, and they went running around trying to help him catch the bird.

When Alcibiades entered public life, Athens was at peace with Sparta, but it was an uneasy peace. Athens and Sparta were the two major powers in Greece, and they had been at war for ten years. The peace had been negotiated by an old general named Nicias. Some leaders in both cities were opposed to the treaty for various reasons, and Alcibiades became one of the leaders of what they called the "war party" in Athens.

Alcibiades made a name for himself as a leader in the Assembly who knew how to win by outsmarting his opponents. He was always holding some kind of secret meetings and setting up secret schemes. He had these secret negotiations with representatives from the cities of Argos, Mantinea, and Elis. These three cities had been allies of Sparta's up until this time. He was able to make a secret alliance with each one of these three cities on behalf of Athens.

Then, when ambassadors from Sparta came to town to try to negotiate a permanent treaty, Alcibiades outsmarted them and undermined the whole peace effort because he didn't believe in it. First, he held a secret meeting with the Spartans and was real friendly and pretended to try to help. His advice to them was to conceal their full power to negotiate. Then, the next day, the ambassadors appeared before Assembly. Pretty soon Alciabides got up and accused the Spartan ambassadors of trying to trick the Assembly. He exposed some details of the deal that they had left out because he had advised them to do just that. He made it look like they were trying to hide something. This stirred up the Assembly members. They stood up and called the Spartan ambassadors all kinds of names and told them to take their lying rear ends back to Sparta. That was the end of any kind of peace deal.

I don't know why Alcibiades was opposed to peace with Sparta. It may have been that he was afraid that Athens might stop building up their military and Sparta would continue to build their army until Sparta was an even bigger threat. Or it could have been personal. Acibiades' grandfather many years before that had been Sparta's trade representative in Athens. When the job had come open a couple of years back, Alcibiades had wanted it. But Sparta had picked somebody else.

INVASIAN OF SICILY

A few months later, something else came up. A proposal was made to the Assembly to send an expedition of troops down to the island of Sicily to take it over and make it part of the Athenian empire. For the past twenty or more years, this idea had been brought up from time to time. Sicily was a large island, and it was rich in natural resources. Best of all, it was located out in the middle of where all that trading that was going on during that time in the Mediterranean Sea. Some of the leaders in Athens were always looking for a way to make Athens a world power, and getting control of Sicily seemed like a smart move, if they could do it. Alcibiades was one of those leaders. He became more and more convinced it was a good idea, and he began to mention it whenever he got the chance.

Then one day the opportunity to really move ahead with this idea fell into their lap. That was the day a delegation arrived from the city of Egesta and presented themselves to the Assembly. Egesta was a barbarian city, which means, of course, that they weren't Greeks. Anyway, Egesta was located on the island of Sicily, and the delegation had come to ask for military assistance in a dispute with one of its neighbors. The Egestaeans even agreed to pay for the expedition.

The Athens Assembly leaders couldn't believe it. They sent representatives back home with the Egestaeans because this would not be a small enterprise, and if they decided to do it, it would be an expensive proposition. They wanted to make sure that the Egestaeans really had enough money to pay for such an expensive enterprise. The representatives came back to Athens several weeks later with sixty talents of silver, and they said that Egesta was indeed a wealthy city.

With that news, Alcibiades stood up and made a motion that they approve the expedition to Sicily. The Assembly voted on it right then, and they voted overwhelmingly in favor of it. Nicias, the old general who had tried to make peace with the Spartans, stood up and spoke against the expedition. He thought it was a crazy idea. He told the Assembly that if Athens shipped the largest part of its army and its navy all the way to Sicily, the city's defenses would be left in a weakened condition. He said that the Athenian soldiers would be fighting in a strange land far away, and that it was too great a risk.

Alcibiades stood up and rebutted Nicias' arguments. He assured the Assembly that allies in Sicily would come to the aid of Athens when they arrived on the island. He said that the people that lived in those cities in Sicily were a bunch of "motley rabble", and that victory over them would be easy. Furthermore, he said, it was a bold move. And it would make Athens look like a world power, and more and more of the smaller states would want to become their allies. He said that the alternative, to sit and do nothing, would mean that other cities around them would become stronger and stronger and Athens would become weaker. He said Sicily would be just the starting point. From there Athens would extend her empire to Carthage and Libya, and to Italy.

Two great scholars, Socrates and Meton, a famous astronomer, stood up and spoke against the proposal. They thought it was too risky. But Alcibiades' visions for the future of Athens had gotten the members of the Assembly all excited. They took a vote on it, and it passed by a large margin.

Now, Athens was a true democracy. Provided you weren't a slave or a woman, of course. All decisions, large and small, that had to do with running the government, whether it was setting the tax rate, building streets or public buildings, or going to war, or making any kind of laws or ordinances, the Assembly voted on it. And the Assembly was made up of all adult male citizens of Athens. It was the first democracy the world had ever known.

So the members of the Assembly didn't want to just turn the whole army and navy over to one man. That would be too much power. So they split the forces among three generals. And it was three generals with very little in common. There was Alciabides, who everybody knew to be young and brash. There was old Nicias, careful and by-the-book and opposed to expedition from the start. And there was Lamachus, another general who was old, but he was know as a vigorous and bold leader.

The three men were commissioned by the Assembly, and they began to meet and make all the necessary preparations for the invasion of Sicily.

MUTILATION OF HERMES

While all the hustle and bustle and preparation for the expedition to Sicily was going on, it came time for the Feast of the

Death of Adonis. This was a big holiday. The celebration always began with a bunch of women marching through the streets carrying images of dead men, wailing as they went. They ended up in this square where they performed a funeral ceremony and pretended to bury the dead men all over again. Some people whispered that this timing was an unlucky omen. They turned out to be right.

Then something happened that really shook the city. One night there were widespread acts of vandalism. Pretty soon the whole thing developed into a crisis that threatened to sidetrack plans for the expedition to Sicily altogether. The incident was called the mutilation of the Hermae. The Hermae were these little short statues of Hermes that stood outside the gates of public parks and a lot of people had them in their gardens or front yards to ward off evil spirits. Hermes was the god who watched over shepherds and travelers. He was the messenger from the gods who guided the souls of the dead to the underworld. Some statues had a big life-size head with a beard and a tiny little body. Others had round hats with wings and wings on his heels. And, since he was the god of fertility, each statue had a prominent penis with a nice set of testicles. Well, it seems that someone went around all over town in the middle of the night and, you guessed it, broke all the penises off.

This was big news the next day. Everyone had his own theory about what happened. Some people thought the deed was done by spies who were trying to delay the expedition to Sicily. Other people said that it was a bunch of rowdy young men who got drunk and were up to no good. A lot of the Greeks were highly superstitious anyway, so the incident sent a chill up everyone's spines, and there was an atmosphere of outrage all over Athens. The Assembly met every day, and the Assembly members stood up and told how offended they were and how determined they were to bring the perpetrators to justice.

In the last days before the fleet was scheduled to shove off, something else happened that rocked Athens and probably changed the course of history. It happened during an important

117

session of the Assembly. Alcibiades, Nicias, and Lamachus were discussing last minute details of the voyage to Sicily, and a member of the Assembly stood up and asked to speak. He was recognized, and he stood up and accused Alcibiades of crimes against the state. He said Alcibiades and his friends had been holding mock celebrations of the Mysteries of Eleusis in a private house. He had his slave brought in, and the slave claimed that he had been an eyewitness. Alcibiades was supposedly playing the role of the high priest and his friends played the parts of the herald and the torch bearer. The rest of the company played the part of new members who were being initiated into this secret organization.

Now, you are probably wondering just what these Eleusinian Mysteries were. Well, it seems that they were a group of festivals associated with sowing a new crop in the fall of the year. Some of the rituals were very elaborate and very complicated.

There were the Little Mysteries in spring and the Great Mysteries in the fall. There were sacred objects concealed in baskets and moved from one chapel to another. There was purification of the candidates and their sacrificial pigs by bathing in the sea. Then there was the ceremony when the pigs were sacrificed. Then there were two days of festival. Then the whole crowd marched in a procession, and transported the sacred objects back to the original chapel.

Anyway, you get the idea. There were the initiation ceremonies with their secret rites. Certain participants played parts that celebrated certain mythological legends. There was fasting during the day and then that night there was feasting on sacred food and drink. Then there was a march through the underworld, and everybody carried a torch. Then there was a symbolic marriage ceremony of the priest and the priestess, and celebrations of death and then rebirth of a child. All this was supposed to symbolize the cycle of the seed produced by the marriage of Heaven and Earth. All these rites were secret, and anyone who participated and then told about it was supposed to be punished.

So you can see, some people took these charges against Alcibiades seriously. And some just didn't like him, and they just wanted to bring him down. The council was told that there was another witness who lived in a town close-by. They sent for him, and he arrived to testify the next day. In a dramatic day of testimony, this witness furnished a list of all the people who participated in the mock celebration of the Mysteries. And, as a bonus, this guy said he knew who mutilated the Hermae. He said it was Alcibiades and his friends.

Then other witnesses came forward to corroborate the testimony. Of course, the members of the Assembly were horrified. Some began to say that the actions by Alcibiades and his friends were part of a conspiracy aimed at overthrowing the democracy.

Alcibiades jumped up, his face turned red, and he hollered that it was all a bunch of lies. He looked all around at the Assembly members' faces, and he couldn't believe that they were actually doubting his word. He was fit to be tied. He told them he wanted a trial right then.

The armada was ready to sail for Sicily, and Alcibiades knew he had the army behind him. He also had the armies from some of the other Greek cities with him. They had threatened to forget the whole expedition if Alcibiades was not one of the leaders. So he knew that a trial would be short and that he would be found not guilty because no one would dare do anything to delay the departure of the fleet.

But the enemies of Alcibiades outsmarted him. They persuaded the Assembly to delay the trial until the military campaign was over and everybody had come back home. You can imagine how upset this made Alcibiades. He was forced to embark on this historic campaign with the cloud of all these accusations hanging over his head.

THE FLEET SAILS FOR SICILY

The big day of the departure finally came. There were big speeches and great fanfare. Mothers cried and children cried and said goodbye to the troops. As the fleet sailed westward, they would be joined by ships sent by various other cities of Greece.

In all, there were 134 warships. Also, thirty merchant ships sailed along with them to bring the food and supplies, and there were more than 100 small boats along with them. The warships were called triremes because they had three decks of people pulling on the oars on each side of the boat. On board the triremes were 5100 hoplites and 1300 other soldiers armed with bows and arrows, slings, and other weapons. All together they had 27,000 people.

MORE ACCUSATIONS

As you might have guessed, after the fleet departed, Alcibiades' enemies were at it again. The Assembly decided to get the investigation started up again, and the more they investigated, the more tales were told. Rewards were offered for testimony. Some members of Athens' leading families were accused and arrested. Some of the accusers were men who everybody knew to be of questionable integrity.

One witness claimed that he was an eyewitness to three hundred men in the public center of Athens late on the night of the mutilation of the Hermae. He claimed he saw all their faces clearly by the light of the moon. Two of the names he named were members of the council who were sitting right there in the chamber. They jumped up and ran down the hall and escaped. Later, somebody mentioned that the mutilations took place on a night when there was no moon.

And from this point, the investigation became even more loud and boisterous, and more people were accused. Andocides, one of Alcibiades' worst enemies in the Assembly, was one of the men accused of being part of the conspiracy. His father and other family members were also accused. People were being executed left and right, so, in desperation, Andocides agreed to testify in exchange for a pardon for himself and for his family. So he gave a full confession to things he didn't do, and he started naming names. The people he named were innocent, and he knew it. He was just afraid for his life, so once he started lying, he just went

120

on and on. Many of the innocent people he accused were executed. He even named some of his own servants, and they were executed.

The public was indignant. They were angry. Pretty soon the Assembly voted to send a delegation of law enforcement officers to catch up with the armada to place Alcibiades under arrest and bring him back for trial. The officers were told to be careful and to use a little finesse in the arrest and not to start a mutiny among Alcibiades' troops.

The fleet had already arrived in Sicily when the officers sent by the Assembly caught up with them. You can imagine how Alcibiades felt when the officers asked him to return to Athens with them to answer new charges. They didn't place him under arrest. They asked that he accompany them peacefully, and he agreed. So when they departed for home, Alcibiades and his crew followed along in his personal ship. Now, the men who rowed the triremes couldn't row for twenty-four hours a day, so back in those days, the ships would pull in somewhere for the night so the crew could get some sleep. When they stopped in a town called Thurii for the night, Alcibiades and his comrades abandoned his ship and escaped over land to Argos, a city where they could hide out with some friends.

Meanwhile, back in Athens, Alcibiades was convicted of treason and condemned to death. His estate and everything he owned was confiscated by the state, and he was put on the most wanted list.

News traveled fast, even in those days, and when Alcibiades heard about it, he snuck out of Argos in the middle of the night headed for Sparta. When he arrived in Sparta, he requested asylum, and the Spartans granted it.

Alcibiades was so angry that he offered to give the Spartans inside information to help them defeat the Athenians. His advice was to take action immediately and to make three strategic moves. First, send reinforcements to Sicily immediately to help Syracuse fight off the invasion of the Athenians there. Second, cut off Athens' access to their silver mines. And third, he advised them to attack the city of Athens itself while most of its army was in Sicily. Most people think that it was Alcibiades' advice to the Spartans that changed the outcome of the war and that led to the downfall of the Athenian Empire.

The so-called Sicilian venture turned out to be a total disaster for Athens. Almost all Athenian soldiers and their allies on this expedition were killed or sold into slavery. This defeat weakened Athens and led to total defeat and the destruction of the Athenian Empire just nine years later.

What's the moral of this story? Your answer is as good as mine, but I would say that sometimes a decision made by emotional members of a democracy can make just as big a mess of things as one made by a dictator or a king. Another one might be that when you make fun of somebody's religion, they can get mad enough to lose their sense of reason and do something crazy to punish you even if it harms them and their whole country.

ROBERT PRINGLE, CHARLES TOWN MERCHANT

Now I'm going to tell you about a man named Robert Pringle. Robert Pringle was an energetic young boy from Scotland who came to Charles Town, South Carolina, in 1725. The town was growing, and there was a lot of trading going on. He got into the trading business and before long he was a rich man. The reason I'm going to tell you about him is that we can see how things were in Charleston back then and how people like him made money and influenced life in America.

First, let me remind you that we don't have to admire these people and agree with how they lived just because I tell you about them. They did a lot of things that I consider mean and foolish and wrong, but that's just the way people were back then.

Now, why would I pick Robert Pringle to tell you about? I'll tell you why. It's because people back then didn't have e-mail and fax machines and telephones. The only ways they had to communicate was to tell you in person or by writing you a letter. And the library at East Carolina University has a copy of all of Robert Pringle's letters in their library, and I sat down over there one day and read some of them. Then I went back the next day and read the rest of them. You can tell a lot about a man by reading his letters.

CIVIL WAR IN ENGLAND

Sometimes it's hard to tell one story without telling part of another story first. Like how North and South Carolina got started. It started in England in 1642. That was when a war broke out. The war was between the members of Parliament and their followers on one side and King Charles and his army on the other.

Parliament and the King had been in a power struggle for many years. The King felt like he was the King and he should rule. Parliament felt that England should be ruled by laws passed by elected members of Parliament.

Both sides used all kinds of tactics. The King disbanded Parliament in 1629. He didn't let them meet any more for eleven years. When they did finally come back and convene in 1640, they stayed in session and refused to take a recess for the next 13 years. Well, war broke out in 1642, and it was a fierce war. It was a civil war, just like the American civil war, only that wouldn't come for 200 more years. Anyway, the war went on and on for six years, and it finally ended when King Charles was captured. Parliament conducted a trial, the King was convicted, and when they passed sentence, the sentence was death. He was executed by having his head chopped off with a big axe.

By the way, part of the disagreement was about religion. Many of the members of Parliament were Puritans, and after the King was executed, the leader of the Puritans, Oliver Cromwell, made himself ruler of England. He made the laws, and his soldiers saw that people obeyed them. And his laws were made according to the Puritan religion such as how people should dress and how men and women should conduct themselves. He closed down all the theatres and made it a crime to do any kind of work on Sunday. He cut out drinking and dancing to celebrate holidays. Needless to say, living under Puritan rule got old in a hurry for many of the English people. A lot of them wished for the old days when they were ruled by the King.

RETURN OF THE KING

That's why, when old Oliver Cromwell died in 1658, some people started asking for King Charles' son, Charles II. He had been hiding out in France all those years. Two years later he loaded his army aboard some ships and sailed back across the English Channel, and when he got there the English people welcomed him and pronounced him King.

Once King Charles had gotten situated and things had settled down, he showed his appreciation for those noblemen who had helped him gain power by giving them grants of land and positions in his government. In 1663, the new King granted a huge parcel of land in North America to eight of his loyal supporters. The eight owners named their new land Carolina. That's Latin for Charles.

The new owners became known in Carolina as the eight Lords Proprietors. I'm going to mention their names because some of these eight names will sound real familiar. They were Edward Hyde, Earl of Clarendon; George Monck, Duke of Albemarle; William, Earl of Craven; Lord John Berkeley and his brother, William Berkley, who was Governor of Virginia;

Sir George Carteret; Anthony Ashley-Cooper; and Sir John Colleton. Today we have Hyde County, Carteret County, and Craven County in North Carolina. There is Berkeley Boulevard and Berkeley Park Mall in Goldsboro, North Carolina, and the Albemarle Sound in the northeast. Then, down in South Carolina, there are the Ashley and Cooper Rivers and Colleton and Clarendon Counties.

NEW SETTLEMENT IN THE WILDERNESS

The first two settlements in South Carolina didn't make it. The settlers got run off by the Indians or they left because they didn't have enough to eat. But then, they finally established a colony at the mouth of the Ashley River. More and more people came there to get free land and to try to start a new life in a new land, and pretty soon they had a good-sized little town. They named it Charles Town. Today, we call it Charleston.

A lot of the settlers came from the tiny island of Barbados down in the Caribbean Sea. Barbados had been settled by English people much earlier, and the people there had learned to grow sugar cane. Sugar caught on all over Europe, and prices went sky-high. So the sugar plantation owners in Barbados became extremely wealthy. They used slave labor to harvest the sugar cane. They were known for being cruel to their slaves. It didn't bother them at all to work people out in that hot sun until they fell over dead. They'd just go out and buy some more slaves.

Pretty soon all the land on Barbados was owned by somebody, and every inch of it had been cleared and planted in sugar cane. And so many people had moved there to try to make money that the island was overcrowded. Some of the Lords Proprietors had land in Barbados, and they decided to try to get people to move from Barbados to South Carolina by offering free land. They offered 150 acres for every man, male servant, and male slave. So the more slaves a man brought with him from Barbados, the more land he got in South Carolina.

People also moved to the area around Charles Town from England, New York, New England, Virginia, Bermuda, and the Bahamas. In some of Robert Pringle's letters, he mentioned how fast Charles Town was growing, even before he got there. In 1690, they had about 4,000 people, and by 1700 they had over 6,000.

HOW THE PEOPLE IN CHARLES TOWN MADE A LIVING

Once people came there and got themselves some free land, they had to find out what would grow there that they could sell and make enough money to feed their families. They tried a little cotton, some indigo, ginger, grapes, and even some olives, but they didn't have much luck. Some people tried growing tobacco, but the quality was not as good as Virginia tobacco.

So they grew hogs and cattle because people ate a lot of meat back then and not too many people ate chicken or turkey. The Charles Town farmers shipped their pork and beef to England and to other colonies. They kept the meat from spoiling by storing it in refrigerated compartments in the ships. What's that? Electricity and refrigerators hadn't been invented yet. You're right. Then how did they store meat back then? The answer is: They soaked it in salt water, and when it dried out they stuffed it into wooden barrels.

They also traded with the Indians for deerskins and furs and turned around and shipped them to England and sold them for a profit. This trade was good at times, but part of the time, the Indians would get mad and stop bringing in the deerskins and furs. That's because some of the white people treated the Indians so badly. In a lot of cases they would cheat them. Sometimes they would rob them or even attack the Indian villages and capture the men, the women, and the children and take them back to Charles Town and sell them for slaves.

HOW RICE AFFECTED CHARLES TOWN

Anyway, some farmers tried growing rice, and they found that it would grow real good in that low, swampy land. Some of the slaves from Africa brought some rice over and were planting it, and the white colonists learned how to grow it from them. When they found our how much money they could make, they got serious and started planting big fields of it. Soon it was the leading crop. Just to give you some idea, Robert Pringle told somebody that around 1720, they had over a million acres in rice, and by 1740, they had two million.

To grow all this rice, the farmers needed a lot of help, and since they didn't have to pay slaves any wages, they began to buy more and more slaves. There have been a lot of books and movies about the terrible way slave traders captured people in Africa and chained them up and brought them to America for sale. Well, Charles Town was a big market for them. They had a big slave market right there in the center of town. Land owners went there to bid on them at the auctions like you would cattle or horses. To give you an idea of how many slaves there were in South Carolina, there were about the same number of slaves as there were white people in 1700. In 1760, there were eight slaves for every white person.

NAVAL STORES

Naval stores became another major export from South Carolina just like they were from North Carolina. Naval stores were products that came from pine trees that were used to build boats and ships and keep them watertight. There was tar and there was turpentine and there was pitch. All three were made from cooking pine sap in big pots. The colonists went out in the woods and cut holes in the pine trees stuck a short piece of pipe in the hole. Then they put buckets under the pipes to catch the sap.

They also made barrel staves. They were flat, curved pieces of wood shaped so that if you fitted them together you could make a barrel. Everything back then was shipped in barrels. They also made long poles to be used for masts.

So you can see why naval stores were so important back then. Think about it. This was the early 1700's and the steamship wouldn't be invented for another hundred years. The railroad wouldn't come along until the 1830's and the pickup truck until the 1890's and the plane until the Wright brothers' flight in 1903.

So back then the only way you could get your produce to a market where you could sell it was to load it in a wagon pulled by a horse or mule or put it in a boat. Since there were no roads or bridges in those early years, boats were the best choice. So all the early farms and plantations were situated next to a river so that traders with boats could come by and stop at the farmer's dock and buy whatever the farmer had to sell. Then they would row or sail down to Charles Town and sell it to some other merchant who would load it on a big ship there in Charles Town harbor and send it across the ocean to be sold in a faraway port. And all these boats and ships were all made of wood. And if any of the boards shrank or warped and sprang a leak or hit a rock and got a hole knocked in it, guess what. Water came in, and you know what happens when water floods into a ship.

So you can see why naval stores were in such demand all over the world. The tar and pitch filled in all the cracks and turpentine kept the wood water-proof. And pine trees didn't grow everywhere, but there were plenty of them in the Carolinas, so a lot of the colonists there made money selling naval stores.

WORLD TRADE CENTERS

And since almost everything produced or manufactured and sold had to be transported by wooden ships, all the products had to be loaded and unloaded at the docks and so the world's seaport cities became the centers of commerce. That's why the biggest cities in the English colonies in America were Boston, New York, Philadelphia, and, of course, Charles Town.

Charles Town was situated where the Ashley River and the Cooper River empty into the ocean. So all the rice, naval stores, and deerskins and furs could be brought down the rivers and loaded on the big trading ships. And there was one other product I forgot to mention. It was indigo. It was a crop used to make dye. It became an important crop whenever England went to war with France and the textile manufacturers couldn't get indigo from the French farmers in the Caribbean islands.

The ships that brought goods into Charles Town and took goods back out were loaded down so that they needed deep water to float out of the harbor. So they had to wait until high tide to set sail. So every day when high tide came, here came ships coming in and ships putting out to sea. Robert Pringle wrote a letter to somebody and told them that 252 ships had entered Charles Town harbor in 1737. That's about five ships a week. That's a lot of unloading and loading. Somebody wrote back and said New York had 243 ships that year, and they thought Philadelphia usually had about 200 every year. About that time Charles Town had about 7,000 people, and New York and Philadelphia each had about 10,000 people.

YOUNG ROBERT PRINGLE

And that brings us to Robert Pringle, the ambitious young man from Scotland who wanted so badly to be rich and important. He had worked in London for a while before he came to Charles Town. He had served as an apprentice to a merchant named Humphrey Hill who imported products from the West

Indies. So when young Robert arrived in Charles Town in 1725, he thought he knew enough about trading to go into business for himself. He bought goods in England and sold them in Charles Town, and he bought goods in Charles Town and sold them in England and other places. That way he collected a commission on cargo coming in and cargo going out. He started off dealing in dry goods. That meant a variety of products such as hats, saddles, linens, nails, pottery, sail cloth, firearms, gunpowder, tobacco, tea, coffee, wine, soap, candles, corn, clothing, citrus fruit, hardware, peas, livestock, and salt.

Over the years he established trading partners in London; Boston; New York; Newport, Rhode Island; and Barbados and in other islands in the Caribbean such as Antigua and St. Christopher. His main contact in London was his brother Andrew. Andrew had been a sea captain before he went into the trading business.

When Robert Pringle had made some money and had a good amount in the bank, he had gotten established enough so he could buy stuff on credit. Then he began to trade in commodities. That's where the real money was. He exported rice, naval stores, and deerskins, and he imported rum, molasses, and sugar.

In 1734 he got married. He married a girl whose father was a Charles Town merchant just like Robert was. Robert's new father-in-law had been in the business a long time, and Robert made a lot of important contacts though him.

TRADING PARTNERS

Robert knew he couldn't operate without his contacts and trading partners, so he was always respectful to them, and he tried to help them out whenever he could. For one thing, he sent them gifts such as a cask of wine every once in a while. He wrote letters to them to keep them informed about the rice crop and other news that might affect prices. And if anybody in Charles Town owed money to any of his friends in far away places, he went out of his way to help them collect their money.

Robert Pringle and his trading partners got to be good friends over the years. They would bring their wives and children to visit each other. A business associate might be on his way from Barbados to London or to Boston and he and his family would stop off in Charles Town and stay a few days with the Pringles.

There was a lot of disease in Charles Town in the summer time. Diseases like yellow fever and malaria. Sometimes Pringle would send his wife and children to stay with his trading partner in Newport, Rhode Island, for several weeks during the summer. A lot of families that could afford it did the same thing. They didn't know about mosquitoes carrying various bacteria and viruses, but they knew something in the hot swampy areas caused it because they didn't have that problem in New England.

Robert tried to help other people in the trading business because he figured you never know when he might need help in their home town. Back in 1739, there was this new guy named Richard Thompson who was trying to get started, and he was doing everything wrong and learning his lessons the hard way. He lived in Hull, in England, and he sent a ship full of goods to be sold in Charles Town. Robert Pringle wrote him a letter and told him that the gun powder, lead shot, nails, hats, gloves, and paint were damaged by the coal that had been dumped on top of them. He also said the grindstones had no holes, the bowls on the tobacco pipes were too small, the hoe handles were too short, and the nails were too small. And the wines didn't taste that good.

On top of that, it was July, and there was no market for coal in July in South Carolina.

And on top of that, there was nothing available to load up for the return trip. The new crop of rice wouldn't be harvested until September or October, and tar and pitch were not available because nobody went out in the woods and did that kind of work in the summer months. It was just too hot.

So Mr. Thompson was in a mess. And Robert Pringle stepped in to help as much as he could. First, he had Thompson's ship towed upstream to fresh water so that the worms that live in the salt water in the harbor wouldn't eat up the hull of his ship.

Then he tried to sell the items in the cargo and get the best price he could.

In the meantime, the ship's captain caught one of those South Carolina lowlands diseases and died. So Pringle had to find Thompson another sea captain and hire him.

Finally, in October, they had his ship loaded with rice from the new crop, naval stores, and deerskins, and it set sail for England. Pringle sent Thompson a bill, but he only charged a two-and-a-half percent commission instead of his usual five percent.

The trading partner that Robert Pringle relied on the most, of course, was his brother, Andrew, in London. If you count his letters, you find out that Robert sent Andrew twenty-five letters in 1742. He sent him thirty in 1743 and twenty-one 1744. That adds up to more than two every month.

Robert was always advising his partners about what they should ship for sale in Charles Town. He told them what the price of commodities such as sugar and rum and pork were. And he told them what products happened to be scarce in Charles Town at the time. He talked about how scarce gunpowder was and also such items as salad oil, Italian wine, and olives. In one letter, he talked about how scarce gold and silver were.

PROBLEMS

Robert Pringle and the other high-flying business tycoons and their trading partners made a lot of money during these times because the Europeans were expanding into new territories all over the world, and wherever Europeans settled, they needed to ship produce back to Europe for sale. And, they needed things from back home that they couldn't get over here in the woods or over in India or down in South America or wherever they were. So somebody had to ship it, and everybody involved got a fee for their services.

But, these entrepreneurs took a big chance every time they sent a ship load of products across the ocean because they never knew when a storm was going to blow up and beat the little ship to pieces. If that happened, they would lose a big pile of money.

Another big problem was all the diseases. Whenever an epidemic broke out, people in other places were scared to send their ships into Charles Town, and the trading business dropped way off. A smallpox epidemic hit Charles Town in the summer of 1737. By then, they knew how to give inoculations, so the epidemic didn't kill many people, but shipping halted anyhow.

Yellow fever and malaria were always a threat, especially to white people when they first arrived from Europe because they had no immunity at all. Pretty soon the word got around Europe and the other colonies that Charles Town was an unhealthy place to live, and the number of immigrants arriving each year dropped off. In fact, some people who lived there moved to other locations. And, like I said before, the rich people sent their families up north or to their friends' plantations in the hilly part of South Carolina for the worse part of the summer.

Hurricanes were another threat that Pringle and his friends had to worry about. Ships out in the ocean and down in the Caribbean were lost during hurricanes, and when they hit Charles Town, they did a lot of damage. Remember, they didn't have airplanes and satellites and radar, so there was no warning.

War and the threat of war breaking out was another problem. If ship owners thought their ship might get attacked by a war ship, they cut back their shipping. And if England was at war with France or Spain, the English Parliament made it illegal to trade with them or their colonies. These slowdowns in shipping made some items scarce, and the prices would shoot way up. And since they couldn't ship their rice out of Charles Town, the price of rice would drop.

Another problem was the Royal Navy of England. They had people like the Shore Patrol whose job was to find sailors in taverns or go aboard ships at the docks and take sailors off these ships. They would take the sailors and force them to join the Royal Navy and serve on navy war ships. They called this practice "impressment." Sometimes they would stop ships at sea and take sailors off of it. They always claimed that the sailors were deserters.

Ships, warehouses, retail shops, and homes were all made out of wood back then, so fire was always a threat. A big fire swept through town in 1740 and almost burned the whole place down. Three hundred homes were burned and a lot of the warehouses and wharves and whatever products were inside were burned. This meant there was nowhere to store the rice crop and no way to load it on ships in the harbor until it could all be rebuilt.

Another problem was the slaves. The slaves outnumbered white people by eight to one. The slaves had no rights at all. They were owned by white people who made them work long hours for no pay. They were mistreated and humiliated. Their children or their wife or husband could be sold off at any time. They lived in poorly built shacks, and sometimes they were fed just enough to keep them alive. They weren't allowed to learn to read or to go hunting or go to church.

So, naturally, they were always angry. They got back at the owners by breaking tools and pretending to be sick or by working real slow. And sometimes they went on the warpath. The newspapers called these attacks insurrections. The most famous one was led by a slave named Nat Turner up around Norfolk, Virginia. He and a band of slaves went from plantation to plantation killing white people. They killed around sixty before they were caught. I read that they let some white people go, though, if their slaves put in a good word for them. This was in 1831.

The same thing happened about twenty miles from Charles Town in 1739. A band of slaves from Stono Plantation killed two guards and stole a bunch of rifles and powder and shot and took off for Florida. A bunch of slaves from other plantations joined up with them along the way. They killed between twenty and thirty white people within the twenty-four hours before they were captured and hung.

This struck fear into the hearts of all slave owners. From then on, white people were afraid to trust their closest servants. All kinds of plots and conspiracies were uncovered. A lot of slaves were whipped or hung whether they were guilty or not.

In 1740, the colonial Assembly decided to take action to see

135

if they couldn't stop having so many slaves brought in to South Carolina. They passed a law that said that if you buy a slave and bring him there within the next three years, you had to pay a tax of 100 pounds. This was a lot of money. When the United States got started forty years later and the department of the treasury began to mint dollars, an English pound was worth about four dollars. So the tax was maybe 400 or 500 dollars a head.

So that's the story of old Robert Pringle and how Charleston got started. His children grew up rich and important in Charles Town society. A hundred years later, the United States was ready to do away with that cruel practice of people owning people, but South Carolinians defended their right to keep slaves along with several other states. Because of this disagreement, South Carolina was the first state to declare that they were no longer going to be a part of the United States. This was the beginning of the Civil War in 1861. The first battle was fought at Fort Sumter in Charleston harbor. But that's another story.

BIBLIOGRAPHY

A Knight's Tale: The Colorful Life and Times of Sir Walter Raleigh and The Shifting Sands of the North Carolina Coast

Lacey, Robert. Sir Walter Raleigh. New York: Atheneum, 1974.

Quinn, David B. Raleigh and the British Empire. London: English University Press, 1947.

Stick, David. Roanoke Island, The Beginnings of English America. Chapel Hill: University of North Carolina Press, 1983.

Thompson, Edward. Sir Walter Raleigh, Last of the Elizabethans. New Haven: Yale University Press, 1936.

Wallace, Willard M. Sir Walter Raleigh. Princeton: Princeton University Press, 1959.

How Louis Brandeis Got Appointed to the Supreme Court

Bryant, H.R.C. "Senate Votes to Confirm Brandeis for High Court." The News and Observer June 2, 1916: 1+.

"America is a Prophecy Says President Wilson." Charlotte Sunday Observer May 21, 1916: 1+.

Daniels, Josephus. The Wilson Era: Years of Peace – 1910-1917. Chapel Hill: University of North Carolina Press, 1944.

Link, Arthur S. Woodrow Wilson and the Progressive Era 1910-1917. New York: Harper, 1954.

"Louis D. Brandeis Named for Place in Supreme Court." The News and Observer Jan. 29, 1916: 1+.

"Brandeis Named for Highest Court; Will be Opposed." The New York Times Jan. 29, 1916: 1+.

"Confirm Brandeis by Vote of 47 to 22." The New York Times June 2, 1916: 1+.

Todd, A.L. Justice on Trial: The Case of Louis D. Brandeis. New York: McGraw-Hill, 1964.

Urofsky, Melvin I. Louis D. Brandeis and the Progressive Tradition. Boston: Little Brown & Co., 1981.

The Short Life of Titus, Emperor of Rome

Garzetti, Albino. From Tiberius to the Antonines: A History of the Roman Empire AD 14-192. Trans. J.R. Foster. London: Methuen, 1974.

Grant Michael. The History of Rome. New York: Charles Scribner's Sons, 1978.

Hadas, Moses, ed. Complete Works of Tacitus. Trans. Alfred John Church and William Joacson Brodribb. New York: Random, 1942.

Jones, Brian W. The Emperor Titus. London: Croom Helm Ltd., 1984.

Josephus. The Jewish War. Trans. G.A. Williamson. New York: Penguin Inc., Penguin Classics; first published Richard Clay Ltd., 1959.

Rajak, Tessa. Josephus. Philadelphia: Fortress Press, 1984; first published Gerald Duckworth & Co. Ltd., 1983.

Suetonius. Trans. J.C. Rolfe. 2 vols. Cambridge, Mass.: Harvard University Press, 1950.

Webster, Graham. The Roman Imperial Army of the First and Second Centuries A.D. Totowa, N.J.: Barnes and Noble Books, 1985.

Stories about Persia

Boyle, John A., ed. Persia: History and Heritage. London: Henry Melland, 1978.

Burn, Andrew Robert. Persia and the Greeks: The Defense of the West, c. 546-478 B.C. New York: St. Martin's Press, 1962.

Frye, Richard N. The Heritage of Persia. Cleveland: The World Publishing Company, 1963.

Herodotus. The Histories. Trans. Aubrey de Selincourt. Baltimore: Penguin Books, 1954.

Olmstead, A.T. History of the Persian Empire. Chicago: University of Chicago Press, 1948.

The Effects of Stalin's Purges on the Soviet People

Conquest, Robert. The Great Terror: Stalin's Purge of the Thirties. Toronto: Macmillan, 1968.

D'Encausse, Helen Carrere. <u>Stalin: Order Through Terror</u>. Trans. Valencee Ionescu. New York: Longman, 1983.

DeJonge, Alex. <u>Stalin: And the Shaping of the Soviet Union</u>. New York: William Morrow, 1986.

Deutscher, I. <u>Stalin: A Political Biography</u>. New York: Oxford University Press, 1949.

Alcibiades and the Fall of the Athenian Empire

Benson, E.F. <u>The Life of Alcibiades: The Idol of Athens</u>. New York: D. Appleton and Company, 1929.

Ellis, W.M. <u>Alcibiades</u>. New York: Routledge, 1989.

Green, P. <u>Armada from Athens</u>. London: Hodder and Stoughton, 1970.

Plutarch. <u>Selected Lives and Essays</u>. Trans. L.R. Loomis. Roslyn, N.Y.: Walter J. Black, Inc., 1951.

Thucydides. <u>The Peloponnesian War</u>. Trans. R. Crawley. New York: Random House, 1982.

Troadec, J.P. "Alcibiades: A Study in Character." Thesis. East Carolina University, Department of History, 1986.

Robert Pringle, Charles Town Merchant

Edgar, Walter B., ed. <u>The Letterbook of Robert Pringle</u>. Volume One: April 2, 1737-Sep. 25, 1742. Volume Two: Oct. 9,

1742-April 29, 1745. Columbia: University of South
Carolina Press, 1972.

McCusker, John J. and Russell R. Menard. <u>The Economy of
British America, 1607-1789</u>. Chapel Hill: University of
North Carolina Press, 1985.

<u>The South-Carolina Gazette</u> 259 Jan. 18, 1739.

<u>The South-Carolina Gazette</u> 260 Jan. 25, 1739.

<u>The South-Carolina Gazette</u> 261 Feb. 1, 1739.

<u>The South-Carolina Gazette</u> 262 Feb. 8, 1739.

<u>The South-Carolina Gazette</u> 326 May17-May24, 1740.

<u>The South-Carolina Gazette</u> 337 Aug. 1-Aug. 8, 1740.

<u>The South-Carolina Gazette</u> 340 Aug. 23-Aug. 30, 1740.

<u>The South-Carolina Gazette</u> 344 Sept. 20-Sept.26, 1740.

<u>The South-Carolina Gazette</u> 357 Dec. 18-Dec. 25, 1740.

<u>The South-Carolina Gazette</u> 459 Jan. 3, 1743.

<u>The South-Carolina Gazette</u> 463 Feb. 7, 1743.

<u>The South-Carolina Gazette</u> 468 March 14, 1743.

<u>The South-Carolina Gazette</u> 475 May 2, 1743.

The South-Carolina Gazette 479 May 3, 1743.

The South-Carolina Gazette 493 Sept. 5, 1743.

The South-Carolina Gazette 498 Oct. 10, 1743.

Weir, Robert M. Colonial South Carolina: A History. Millwood, N.Y.: KTO Press, 1983.